MINE THIS TIME

A Standalone Novel

J.H. CROIX

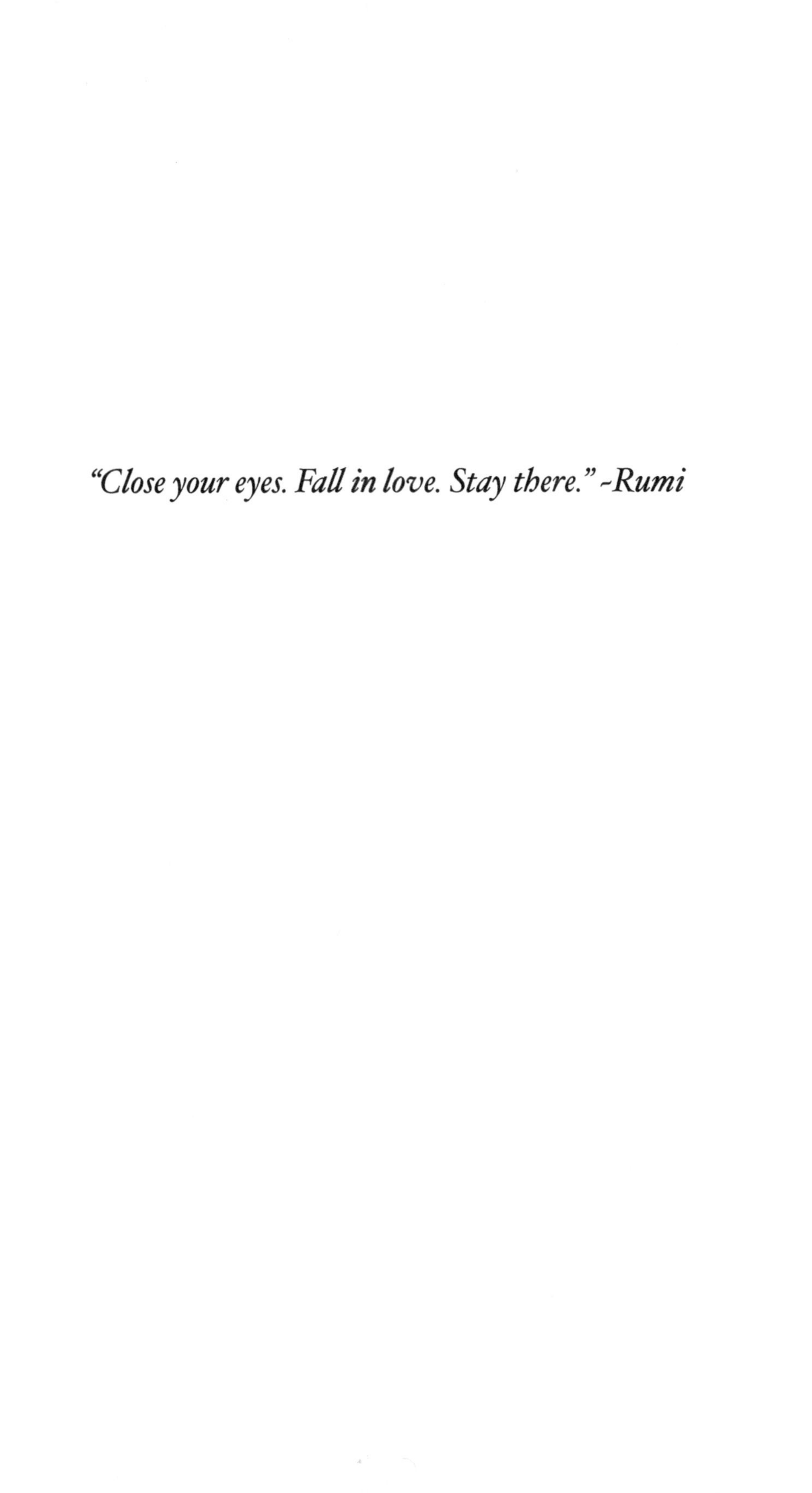

"Close your eyes. Fall in love. Stay there." -Rumi

PREFACE

An earlier version of Mine This Time (formerly titled Easy This Time) was previously included in The Kristen Proby Boudreaux Universe. It was available in Kindle Unlimited for a limited time and has been out of publication since Dec 31, 2021. This is an updated version with all references to The Kristen Proby Boudreaux Universe removed and some other minor changes to the work.

For additional clarification, J.H. Croix has always owned the full copyright to the work, however The Kristen Proby Boudreaux Universe had the rights for publication only for a period of time. Publication rights fully reverted to this author, J.H. Croix, effective Dec 31, 2021.

While this is a standalone novel, Mari Channing is the sister of Max Channing from Melt With You in the Into The Fire Series.

Chapter One

MARI (MARIANA)

Rolling over in bed, I reached my arm reflexively for the man I expected to find, but the sheets were cold under my palm. Alarm punctured my sleep-hazed mind, and I sat up abruptly. Brushing my tangled hair away from my face, I shifted from sleepy to startlingly awake as I scanned the room. I couldn't say why, but somehow, I knew something was seriously off.

"Brett?"

My voice practically echoed in the lovely room at the bed & breakfast where we were staying. Kicking the sheets away, I swung my feet off the bed and walked toward the bathroom, my eyes noticing the distinct lack of my boyfriend's belongings in the room. Last night, his suit jacket was thrown over the chair by a small desk in the corner of the room, and his shoes had been by the door. Both were missing now. Anxiety spun in tight circles in my chest.

"Brett?"

Now I was repeating myself. I hated when I did that.

The tile floor in the bathroom was cool under my feet—no Brett in here. My eyes swung to the vanity. I expected to see Brett's razor because he usually left it by the sink. My toothbrush looked lonely there. By this point, my heart was thudding hard and fast, and my stomach felt as if I were falling from a great height.

Ridiculous as it was, I actually pushed back the shower curtain. As if I might find Brett standing in the shower without the water running. To make more of a fool of myself, I hurried out of the bathroom, my bare feet getting colder by the moment, and opened the door to the single closet in the room.

No Brett in the closet.

I snatched my phone off the desk and pulled up his number. Tapping the screen to call, I held the phone to my ear. "We're sorry. The number you have called is no longer in service."

"What the fuck?!" I exclaimed to the automated operator voice.

Convinced it must be a mistake, I tried again, only to get the same message.

Tossing the phone on the bed, I raced to the

closet and yanked on a pair of jeans, my bra, and a T-shirt. I didn't even bother to check my appearance before running out the door. It was only when I practically skidded to a stop by the dining room of the inn that I realized I hadn't even put on my shoes.

Hannah Grantham happened to be pouring a cup of coffee and glanced over her shoulder. If she was startled at my unkempt, literally rolled-out-of-bed-and-yanked-some-clothes-on look, it didn't show. But then, my brief interaction with her yesterday afternoon had demonstrated she had excellent manners.

"Good morning, Mari," she said smoothly. "How are you this morning?"

Frazzled. Confused. Angry. Upset. Possibly heartbroken.

I had no good answer that was truthful. That said, the way my brain inserted "possible" before heartbroken gave me pause. But, I had more pressing matters at the moment.

"Um, I'm not sure. You didn't happen to see my boyfriend this morning, did you?"

The word boyfriend felt strange coming out. With our work schedules, we hadn't had much time together lately. Okay, hardly any. So little, I'd started to question if I could even call him my boyfriend.

A line formed between Hannah 's brows as she

looked at me. After a long pause, she replied, "No, I haven't."

I stood there, feeling foolish. After a moment, I nodded. "Okay. Thanks."

Turning, I stared down at my toenails as I walked, the deep red polish taunting me with every step. Hannah's voice halted me.

"Would you like some coffee?"

Considering I'd just been wishing I'd never woken up, perhaps not. But then, coffee might be the only thing that could help me think clearly. Turning back, I tried a smile, but it came out shaky. I prayed she didn't notice. "That would be wonderful."

Hannah smiled in return and held a finger up. "Give me just a sec." She hurried through a doorway into the kitchen I'd seen only a glimpse of last night when we checked into this lovely inn near the Mississippi River.

I let my eyes travel out the windows, taking in the area. Tall oak trees lined the driveway with others scattered around the property. Spanish moss hung from the trees, swaying lightly in the breeze. The glint of sunshine glimmering on the nearby creek shimmered in the morning light. Last night, I could smell the jasmine blooming. Just now, with a window open in the dining room on this late spring morning, the breeze carried in scents of flowers and rich greenery. Dew glimmered on the grass where the sun's first rays were cresting above the trees and casting a swath of light at an angle across the lawn.

If I stared out the windows long enough, maybe I could forget that things felt awfully wrong this morning. The comforting view could soothe me, but only so much.

Turning away from the windows, my heart tumbled along in a rapid beat, and I felt slightly ill. Brett had sweet-talked me into coming on this weekend escape even though I'd fretted I didn't have the money, nor the time. He'd been so persistent that I'd somehow convinced myself he had something special planned. I didn't know what that "special" would be, especially with how things had been with us lately.

When we'd arrived yesterday, it had all felt rather magical, and I'd allowed myself to relax in a way I hadn't in months. Creek's End Inn was a gorgeous place. With Hannah so warm and welcoming, and her young son so cute as he took us on a little tour, it was a welcome respite.

My eyes landed on a clock above the doorway into the kitchen. It wasn't even six a.m. yet. It made no sense for Brett to be gone. When we'd gone out to dinner last night, I'd wished things had felt more stable with Brett and me. Because, long before this morning, I'd been harboring doubts about us. Yet I couldn't have imagined he'd abscond during the night.

"We have sugar and cream right over there," Hannah said, gesturing toward a sidebar against the wall in the dining area as she returned to the room with a cup of coffee in hand.

"Neither," I replied, marveling at how manners could get me through this awkward moment when I didn't know where my boyfriend had gone, and his phone was disconnected.

Hannah handed me a mug, one with Creek's End Inn written on the side in a whimsical script. I curled my fingers around it, realizing then my hands were ice cold. I took a sip of coffee, the rich dark brew grounding me slightly. Swallowing, I met her eyes.

"Thank you. This is delicious," I said, quite honestly.

"Glad to hear it. If I can get you anything this morning, please let me know. We serve breakfast within the hour. If you need, I can check to see if anything is ready a little early."

"Oh no, I don't want to be a bother. Is it okay if I carry my coffee up to my room?"

"Of course it is! Do let me know if you need anything else."

I managed a nod, still too shocked to even cry. Although I didn't even know if I needed to cry. Perhaps it was all a misunderstanding.

After I climbed the stairs and closed the door to the room I was supposed to be sharing with Brett, I sank my hips onto the edge of the bed and took a gulp of my coffee.

"Riiiight. Brett just took all his stuff and left and turned off his phone by accident," I whispered to the room.

I wasn't quite sure what was happening. I swung between poles of anger and crushing humiliation. Glancing around, I found my phone where I had tossed it on the bed before my mad dash out of the room. I lifted it, once again tapping on Brett's number.

My gut was telling me Brett was long gone, but I still tried to call him. And I got the same automated message. It felt as if the computerized voice on the other end of the line was mocking me.

Although I was frazzled and in shock, I went through the motions of getting ready. I had no idea what to do if Brett hadn't paid for our stay here. If he hadn't, I was thoroughly screwed.

After a shower, I dressed in a pair of lightweight capris and a flowy cotton blouse, the kind that wouldn't stick to my skin in this humid Louisiana weather. Standing in front of the bathroom mirror, I stared at myself. My dark hair was still damp from the shower, but I didn't have it in me to bother trying to style it. My blue eyes stood out against my rather pale skin. Considering the state of my mind this morning, I supposed I didn't look too bad. With a sigh, I turned away from my reflection.

In between wondering where the hell Brett was, I contemplated how to tactfully ask if he'd paid for the room. I did *not* want to humiliate myself further in front of Hannah, but I had to find a way to ask. Of all the people to be so embarrassed in front of, I didn't want it to be Hannah. She had a fairy-tale life with her two children and her professional basketball player husband—a man who had plenty of women drooling over him—but whose eyes remained fixed only on her, if the occasional gossip reports had it right.

If I was beyond desperate for money, I could always call my brother—Max Channing. Max was my older brother who I adored, but who also drove me slightly crazy with his overbearing ways. He was a wealthy tech investor. He could buy this inn and then some if the fancy struck him. Yet my pride was *not* going to let me call him. I sure as hell didn't want to tell him he was right about Brett.

Don't panic. Maybe Brett's coming back.

Riiiight. That's why he took everything with him, left in the middle of the night, and disconnected his phone.

I could battle inside my head all day, but it didn't change the facts of my situation. Brett appeared to be long gone, and I was damn close to broke. With a sigh, I mentally swatted at my always willing-and-ready-to-be-critical voice. Standing from the bed, I steeled myself. I might as well find out if Brett had paid for the room. Then I could problem-solve.

Moments later, I was relieved to discover Hannah had left to take care of some errands. It was quiet downstairs, and I figured the other guests would soon be making their way down for breakfast. I would be humiliating myself to Hannah 's staff, rather than her. It still sucked, but it was a little bit better.

Approaching a woman carrying a tray of food to the sideboard in the dining room, I said, "Excuse me."

"Yes?"

I smiled tightly, feeling like my face might crack from the effort. "Um, my boyfriend had to leave unexpectedly." Okay, I wasn't totally lying there. Seeing as *I* didn't expect it, Brett's departure could count as unexpected even if he'd planned it. "I didn't have a chance to check with him to find out if he had already taken care of the room for the weekend. I didn't want to let that detail get away from me."

All true. Little did she know my boyfriend had fled during the night, and I didn't know where the hell he was.

The woman smiled warmly. "Give me just a sec." She set down the platter in her hands before waving for me to follow her down the hallway to the reception desk.

She tapped on the screen of a laptop, her eyes scanning for a moment before she looked up. "It doesn't look like it. You can take care of it when you check out," she said, gesturing carefully with her hand. "We hope you'll stay through the weekend even though he couldn't. We're around if you need anything."

I swallowed. Finally, I thought I might cry. I knew I was well and truly screwed. Now, I had my choice of humiliation. Either I called my older brother, or I revealed the situation to Hannah. The idea of leaving today and not coming back flitted through my thoughts. I couldn't do the inn equivalent of dine and dash, though. That was just *not* okay.

Chapter Two

NASH

"Who?"

"Mari Channing," Lydia, my personal assistant, replied.

I didn't recognize the name. "What does she need?"

Lydia shrugged, pursing her lips before adding, "She's rather insistent and would like to meet with you."

I glanced at my watch. "I only have five minutes."

"As if I'm not aware of that, Nash," Lydia replied, her lips quirking slightly in a smile.

Lydia's smiles were rare. She tended to have a rather severe look with her close-cropped silver hair and whip-thin build. With nothing more than a narrowing of her eyes, she could make one think twice if she disapproved. Although I was technically her boss, I was under no illusions. Without her, my business wouldn't be what it was.

I leaned back in my chair, crossing my arms. "Now, Lydia, you don't usually let anyone screw up my schedule. What in the world did Mari Channing say to persuade you that this interruption was worthwhile?"

Lydia stepped into my office, pulling the door closed behind her with a distinct click. "She's looking for Brett Henson."

"Oh, that idiot. Did she say why?"

Brett, or rather the "idiot" as I'd just called him, had asked me about an investment opportunity for a restaurant in New Orleans. He'd lied through his teeth, and I fucking knew it. He was a name-dropper if I'd ever met one. I'd unceremoniously escorted him from my office this morning after he showed up unannounced.

"You know how I draw up a profile on anyone who wants to meet with you about investment opportunities?" Lydia prompted.

I didn't get to where I had in business and investments without being smart about it. When Brett initially contacted my company about an investment opportunity via email, I immediately did my homework. I declined meeting with him as a result. But then, he showed up like an ass. He was arrogant with just enough polish to maybe fool someone less suspicious than me.

"Yes. I scanned the information you found and declined to schedule a meeting with him. But you knew that. Lydia, you know practically every moment of every day of my life," I replied.

Lydia's brown eyes twinkled. "Obviously. I know what happened with Brett. But you might not have noticed the name of his girlfriend. Mariana Channing. She goes by Mari, and her older brother is Max Channing."

My eyebrows hitched up. "Interesting. I didn't catch that detail. I was mostly focused on the financials and skipped the personal info. What in the world could she want?"

"I'm not sure, but I thought you should speak with her."

"I'd guess Max saw right through Brett as well. I'm also guessing Brett hooked up with Mari thinking she might be a path for him to Max and other useful contacts," I mused.

Lydia simply shrugged. "Shall I bring her in?"

"Of course. Now I'm more curious than anything. Call ahead to my lunch meeting and let them know I might be late." Fortunately, the lunch meeting in question was nothing critical.

Moments later, Lydia had exited my office and returned, holding the door open and gesturing for Mari

Channing to enter. I stood from my desk, rounding it to approach Mari. I'd seen many beautiful women in my life, but Mari took my breath away. She had glossy dark curls that fell in a loose tumble around her shoulders. Her blue eyes were like the ocean, the rich blue deep and layered. She had a smattering of freckles on her cheeks, and her nose turned up at the end. Her mouth was slightly crooked, and her lips were plump.

Nothing was remarkable about the way she dressed, as she wore just a pair of capris and a loose blouse. My eyes dipped down to the shadowed valley between her breasts, taking in the amber hue of her skin. My body tightened in response as I approached her, and I distantly marveled at this.

"Nash Reynolds," I said when I reached her, holding my hand out reflexively.

"Mari Channing. Thank you for seeing me," she replied, her palm cool in mine.

I felt a subtle tremor running through her, and concern pricked at me. Releasing her hand, I gestured to a pair of chairs by the windows that looked out over the Mississippi River.

I was unaccountably concerned about Mari. I hadn't gotten to where I had in life without being able to read people well, and I knew beyond a shadow of a doubt that she was distressed. When I glanced toward Lydia at the motion of the door, she mouthed, "Be nice," right before closing it.

I rolled my eyes. Obviously, I was going to be

nice to Mari. I might've thought her boyfriend was an idiot, but she'd done nothing to imply she was. Plus, I knew her brother through our business endeavors and considered him nothing other than entirely upstanding.

"Have a seat," I said when she hesitated.

Mari sat in one of the chairs, smoothing her hands over her thighs. She then clasped them together on her knees as she crossed her legs. Her fingers laced together, tightly enough that I knew she was barely holding it together.

My curiosity was growing by leaps and bounds, but so was my concern. "Can I get you anything? I have coffee right here in the office if you'd like some."

Her laugh was sharp. "No, thank you."

"Well then, what can I do for you?"

"I understand you met my boyfriend, Brett Henson, this morning. I was wondering if you happened to know where he was."

Interesting. Apparently, *she* didn't know where he was. I elected to go for a direct approach. I found that it often saved a lot of time.

"I certainly don't. But considering you're aware he met with me this morning, I would imagine you could figure out where he was."

Mari's nostrils flared as she considered me. Pink bloomed on her cheeks. "Mr. Reynolds——"

"Please call me Nash," I drawled.

Her lips tightened in a line before she nodded. "Nash, then. Brett brought me here for a weekend, and now he's gone. Gone, *gone*, if you understand my meaning. His phone is shut off, and I can't reach him. I also learned the last day on the lease at his condominium was yesterday. As far as I can tell, he's left me. I can deal with that, but I have a few loose ends to tie up, and I'd like to reach him."

Brett was more of an idiot than I'd assumed. To be fool enough to leave Mari Channing at all, much less in this manner, was beyond stupid.

"I'm sorry to tell you, but I don't know where he is. How in the world did you find out he had a meeting with me today? It wasn't a scheduled meeting. He barged in and demanded to talk with me. Considering that my assistant wasn't even here yet, I gave him a few minutes of my time before tossing him out."

Mari leaned back in her chair, releasing her death grip on her knees. "Are you serious?" she asked sharply.

"Quite. If I understand you correctly, it sounds as though he's left you high and dry?"

Those stunning blue eyes met mine, flashing with anger as she stood. "Yes. That asshole."

I mulled over the situation for a moment, surprising myself when I spoke. I usually planned things through, but then Mari seemed to tap into a vein I didn't even know I had. I wasn't about to let her walk out of my office. Not right now.

"If you'd like me to find him, I can certainly do that."

Mari spun back, her brows arching in question. "You can?"

"Of course. Tracking people down is something I do as part of security for my business, and I have a friend who's a private investigator. He can usually sniff out someone who's trying not to be found. Your Brett—"

She cut me off, slicing her hand through the air sharply. "He is *not* my Brett." Her gorgeous eyes flashed again, a restrained passion simmering in their depths.

"Okay, then. Not *your* Brett. Nonetheless, I can still help you find him."

She stared at me, catching her bottom lip in her teeth and utterly distracting me for a moment. I gave myself a mental shake, a hard one. I wasn't prone to offering help, nor was I susceptible to being drawn to any woman this easily.

Her shoulders rose and fell as she took a deep breath, letting it out with a soft sigh. "I don't really know if I want to find him."

Leaning forward, I rested my elbows on my knees. "No? Then what are you doing at my office looking for him?"

Mari's eyes narrowed, her gaze coasting over my

face. "I don't know. He's just gone, and I guess I thought perhaps I could find him. I'm not so sure it's worth it."

She turned away to look out the windows, and I stood. With the way the chairs were situated, angled toward each other, we were perhaps a foot apart. Her scent drifted to me, musky with a hint of vanilla.

Everything in me tightened, and it felt as if the air around us was sparking with electricity. I didn't know what was going to happen, but I knew I didn't want Mari to walk out of this office. If that happened, I might never see her again.

None of this was the least bit rational. I prided myself on being a completely rational person, even in personal matters. So much for that when it came to Mari.

"I suppose I'll go then. Thank you for your time," she said with a slight hitch in her voice.

"Let me at least get you lunch," I heard myself saying.

Those blue eyes widened in surprise, her mouth opening slightly. "Oh, that's not necessary. I—" Her stomach growled, quite audibly. Her cheeks flushed again, and she rolled her eyes. "I promise, my stomach isn't actually trying to answer the question for me."

My lips quirked in a smile. "I wouldn't presume that. But I insist. Let me take you to lunch."

I elected not to let her think too hard about this by turning and sliding my hand down her back, then nudging her forward slightly. Conveniently, there was a light knock on my office door right then, and Lydia opened it. I considered it convenient because it interrupted Mari's chance to brush me off too quickly.

"I was just checking to see what your plan was for lunch. You have a call on line one from Danny Kent," Lydia said.

Danny happened to be one of the men I was supposed to be joining for lunch. I nodded to Lydia as I began walking across the office with Mari following at my side. "You can let Danny know I'll give him a call this afternoon, and that I need to cancel for today. Mari and I are having lunch."

MARI

I looked across the table at Nash Reynolds and willed my pulse to slow. I told myself my reaction to him was simply because I was so out of whack this morning. I mean, I *had* woken up to my boyfriend's abrupt disappearance. It was fair to say I was discombobulated.

I'd scouted out Nash when I pulled up the online calendar I only had access to on my phone because Brett had once logged in on my phone to update it. If I was wondering whether he was trying to cut me out, that was promptly confirmed. A few minutes after I opened it, the app unceremoniously logged me out with a warning that the password had been updated. I was pissed, but those few minutes had given me enough time to find a few trails to follow, starting with the one that led to Nash's office.

There I sat across from Nash Reynolds in a charming little café with a lovely view of Bourbon Street. I'd come close to turning down his lunch invitation, but the truth was I was so hungry I was almost shaking. Although the breakfast at Creek's End Inn looked delicious, I hadn't had much appetite this morning.

Whether it was low blood sugar, or how rattled I was in reaction to Nash, I was ravenous at this point. I took a sip of my water and reached for a sweet potato fry. Nash had ordered them before we even sat down. It was lightly battered and the perfect combination of salty and sweet as I bit into it. I didn't realize a little moan escaped until Nash arched a brow, one corner of his mouth hitching up.

"Good, aren't they?" he teased lightly.

I felt my cheeks heat. "Good isn't enough. Delicious is more fitting."

"Everything here is excellent." Nash glanced up when our waiter arrived at our table again.

"Do you two need a few more minutes?" the young man asked politely.

Nash looked over at me, cocking his head to the side.

"What do you recommend?" I asked, glancing at the waiter.

"Today's special, shrimp with bacon and grits, is a favorite."

"I'll vouch for that. It's my favorite," Nash

replied, the subtle twang to his voice sliding over me like honey.

"I'll take that then." I handed over the menu. I'd hardly been able to focus on the menu, not able to absorb much of anything.

When Nash slid his menu to the edge of the table, the waiter immediately picked it up. "I'll take the same. Would you like some wine with that?" Nash asked, glancing at me.

"Oh, no," I said, shaking my head quickly. "I'm driving."

I sensed Nash had many questions, but he didn't ask them. As the waiter turned away, another man approached our table. He appeared to be a businessman, dressed in slacks and a button-down shirt with the sleeves rolled up. He nodded to me before his gaze swung to Nash. "How are you doing, Nash? Any updates on the issues with that project?"

As Nash began to reply, I tuned it out because I didn't need to listen. Instead, I took a moment to let myself soak in the view of Nash. His hair was dark gold with light streaks as if kissed by the sun. His skin was burnished bronze with his hazel eyes standing out in contrast. His eyes were mesmerizing —a swirl of green, gold, and brown. The depth of color was intense. His features were bold with defined cheekbones, his nose sharp and straight, a strong square jaw, and sensual lips.

There was no doubt he was well built as his

shoulders filled out his button-down shirt that was paired with faded black jeans. Although he wore the casual business look well, he had a restrained energy to him. As if he could throw that polished look off in a flash and his raw, potent masculinity would burst forth.

I imagined he had plenty of women chasing after him. I couldn't say I was particularly familiar with Nash Reynolds, but I knew his name. With my older brother deep into tech investments and tendrils connecting him to various businesses all over the world, I knew he'd been involved in security planning on the tech side for Nash's sprawling real estate investments in New Orleans. Rumor had it the man owned half of this Southern city.

It was only when I heard Nash saying, "You have a good afternoon now, Johnny," and his gaze swung back to me that I realized I'd been staring.

When Nash's gaze collided with mine, my pulse lunged, and my belly spun. Once again, I felt my cheeks get hot. I tried to tell myself I was rattled from such a bizarre morning, but my body wasn't buying that argument.

"So," Nash drawled, "do tell me what brought you to my office looking for not-your-Brett this morning, Mari?"

I traced my fingertips around the water glass set on the dark wooden table. For a moment, I considered coming up with some sort of explanation that wasn't humiliating. But the reality was, I was well and done with Brett after his little stunt, so there was no sense in lying.

"Well, we came down for a weekend stay at a bed & breakfast. It was supposed to be a nice getaway because we've both been really busy. Now, he's gone, and I have no idea where he is. He didn't even pay for our stay, and I'm flat broke. To make a long story short, he's an asshole. I thought perhaps I could track him down and at least give him hell. But it's probably best if I let the whole thing go."

Nash's gaze held mine as he shook his head slowly. "I suppose I'm glad to know you've seen his true colors."

"Oh, did you know Brett? I mean, beyond seeing him this morning."

"I only met him this morning. Before he showed up unannounced, he reached out about an investment opportunity. As I do with any possible investments, I did some looking into his assets and discovered everything was fluff. I declined to meet with him, but he showed up anyway. I gave him five minutes and escorted him out. I can't say I know him personally, but I can tell you his finances are nothing more than a game of smoke and mirrors."

I stared at Nash, anger churning in my gut. Not anger with Nash, mind you. But fury with Brett. I might not know Nash Reynolds well, but I knew he had the resources to assess Brett's supposed financial wizardry. If he thought it was all fluff, it likely was.

"You're telling me—" I closed my eyes and shook my head. After a slow breath, I looked over at Nash. I felt like an idiot. "Never mind. It doesn't really matter in the end. I'll enjoy my lunch and get on with my life."

Nash's gaze swept over my face. It felt as if he could see right into me. Considering the events of the morning, I felt far more vulnerable than I preferred. Complicating matters was my body's reaction to Nash. My body tingled under his intent focus, and a subtle heat suffused me. On the heels of a deep breath, I reached for my water and took another gulp.

Although I'd just blurted out the humiliating truth of my situation, Nash didn't know the compounding layers of history behind it. When I had first started dating Brett, my older brother—my bossy, far too together, older brother—hadn't liked him. Not one bit. In fact, Max had said he thought Brett was using me.

Because I could be stubborn, and because I didn't want to believe Brett had been using me, I'd ignored Max's opinion and continued dating Brett. It had only been a year, but the doubts sown by Max's initial perception had never dissipated. As it was, Brett and I had drifted apart and hardly seen each other for the last few months.

This morning was a spectacular example of why Max had been exactly right. Blessedly, Nash was gracious enough not to push the subject any further. Another interruption from yet another business acquaintance of his gave me enough time to finish eating while he made small talk about some project in New Orleans.

Meanwhile, I was doing mental math, trying to calculate how I could scrape together the funds to cover the bill at Creek's End Inn. I figured I was going to have to put it all on a credit card and hope for the best. When our waiter arrived, she asked if it was one check.

"Oh, no," I replied, shaking my head.

Nash arched a brow before glancing at the waitress. "One check, please."

"I can get my own lunch," I insisted.

Nash stared at me, once again, his gaze feeling like an X-ray on my brain. I mentally battened down the hatches and pulled my pride into place, tattered though it was.

"Mari," he finally began. "I would cover lunch with whomever I brought to lunch. I invited you, so that's what I expect to do."

I managed a shallow breath, willing the spin of emotions inside me to settle. "I can still cover my own lunch." I had no idea why I was arguing about this. Given my financial situation, allowing Nash to take care of the bill was the sensible thing to do. But then, I wasn't feeling particularly sensible.

Nash inclined his head before shrugging. "If you'll excuse me, I'm going to run to the restroom. I'll be right back."

Our waiter nodded and turned away to check on a table nearby when Nash stood, his stride long and confident as he walked across the restaurant. I told myself not to notice the way his shoulders filled out his shirt, not to linger on the way the faded denim of his jeans hugged his muscled legs, and certainly not to acknowledge that the man had one *fine* ass.

What the hell are you doing ogling another man right now? In the last few days, you were all worked up thinking you and Brett might get back on track.

Um, back on track? You mean like sex for the first time in over three months? You didn't even have sex last night.

I couldn't decide which voice was more critical. My proper, try-to-do-life-right voice, or my more sarcastic tone, always on the ready to point out just how ridiculous things were.

True story: I couldn't recall the last time I had sex with Brett.

Nash returned before the waiter did. He stopped by the table and glanced down at me. "Shall we go?"

"Our waiter hasn't brought our checks."

"I've taken care of it."

I felt my nostrils actually flare as I looked up at Nash. "Wow. So you're that kind of overbearing gentleman," I muttered as I reached for my purse.

Nash, being the gentleman in question, pulled my chair back as I stood, not even deigning to offer a reply.

I told myself I most certainly didn't notice the way his warm touch felt like a hot brand on my low back when he placed his palm there as a group of people passing by jostled me. Flutters spun in my belly, and the heat from his touch radiated outward. I was so flustered by my response to him, and my annoyance with my entire day, I elected to pretend everything was fine.

Once we were outside on the sidewalk, I looked up at him. "Thank you for lunch."

I didn't bother to argue about the bill. There was no sense in it. I really didn't have the money to cover my lunch. It would've gone on the credit card that was about to be maxed out if it wasn't already.

"Anytime," Nash replied. "Where are you heading now?"

I bit back the urge to tell him it was none of his damn business. I did have some manners, after all.

"I'll be heading home. Thank you for at least filling me in on what you know about Brett. It was" —I paused and then shrugged—"illuminating."

"My offer still stands."

"Excuse me?" I asked, confused by what he meant.

"To help you find Brett."

I mulled it over for a beat before replying, "I appreciate your offer, but I don't think there's much point in trying to find Brett. It's best for me to move on."

Chapter Four

MARI

"Dammit!" I muttered to myself as I glanced down to see that one of the wheels on my small suitcase had cracked. No wonder it wasn't rolling smoothly.

"Mari," a voice said. A voice I instantly recognized. What was it about Nash Reynolds? Just the sound of his gravelly drawl sent butterflies spinning in my belly.

The hot Louisiana sun beat down on me. The humid air was so heavy it felt as if it was sticking to my skin. Lifting my head, I unconsciously smoothed my hand over my hair. It was pulled back into a messy ponytail. The state of my hair was representative of how I felt about my life. I couldn't seem to keep anything tidy.

Straightening, I turned and pasted a smile on my face. "Hello, Nash."

With the sun glinting on his bronze hair, Nash inclined his head slightly. "Hello, Mari. How are you?"

I curled my hand more tightly around my suitcase handle and hoped I could fake my way through this. Because the truth was, I was *not* well, not one bit. Unbeknownst to me until yesterday morning, Brett had also run up all my credit cards to the limit. Hannah Grantham had been gracious enough to insist that I needn't worry about the bill. Whether it was because she could tell I was on the verge of tears or not, I fully intended to find a way to take care of it as soon as I could.

I was mortified and utterly horrified at the situation in which I found myself. In fact, I was so embarrassed that I'd considered calling my brother and his wife, Harlow, for help. But alas, they were out of the country traveling this week. Max, of course, would help with anything I needed, but I didn't want to stoop to that. I would get myself out of this situation on my own one way or another.

With my polite smile stuck on my face, I lied through my teeth in reply. "I'm well, and yourself?"

Nash began to say something, but in the bustle of people on the sidewalk outside the airport, someone bumped into me and sent me colliding into him. I looked up to find his eyes on me. His body was all hard planes. He had one arm wrapped around my waist, steadying me as my hand fell against his chest.

My heartbeat went wild, thudding furiously inside the cage of my ribs. My breath became short as heat spun like fire through my veins.

"I'm just fine," he said, not missing a beat in the conversation.

This was the point when I should've moved away. But I found myself frozen, savoring the feel of his strength and wanting to surrender to it and stop trying so hard to do this all on my own.

"Where are you headed?" Nash asked as he stepped back.

It said something about the state of my body that I experienced a flash of yearning at the loss of his warm strength pressed against me even if it was only by accident. I met his gaze, ignoring the hum of my racing pulse rippling outward through my body. "I'm flying back to San Francisco," I said.

Nash looked at me quietly for several long beats before nodding. "Okay then. You know where to reach me if you decide you want some help chasing down Brett."

"I do. I appreciate your offer. I'll think about it."

"Please do." Just two words, but the way he said them in that slow drawl that slid over me like sweet molasses sent my belly spinning and made my breath catch in my throat.

"Thank you again for lunch the other day," I rasped.

Dear God. This man was literally taking my breath away.

"You're most welcome, Mari. Give your brother my best."

I managed a tight smile. I forced my feet to move because I couldn't let myself get caught in the quicksand of Nash's melting hot eyes. They made my body go a little crazy.

Without another word, I hurried past him, ignoring the rhythmic thump of the broken wheel on my suitcase. Nash couldn't know it, but the sound of that wheel only added to the layers of embarrassment I was experiencing. I felt flustered inside and out and was beyond mortified at my circumstances. I was just praying that Brett hadn't discovered the one credit card I'd never touched and kept as a backup.

At least I had a return ticket home. The sooner this stupid "getaway" ended, the better.

———

"Excuse me?" I asked, trying to quell the sinking feeling in my stomach.

The contrast of the humid Louisiana heat to the cold air conditioning inside the airport only served to amp up how unsettled I felt. My encounter with

Nash had gotten me hot and bothered. I'd already been hot and sticky, and then I came in here to the blast of icy air, and my sweat dried on my skin almost instantly.

Now, my hands were shaking, and my fingertips were tingling from the cold. The woman clicked a key on her keyboard before looking up at me. "Your return ticket was refunded to the purchaser," she said.

I opened my mouth to reply but snapped it shut. I was afraid I might scream. I fumbled for my purse and yanked out my wallet. Looking up, I passed over my credit card. "I just need a ticket back to San Francisco. I'm hoping I can make my originally scheduled flight." I was kind of amazed I managed to speak, but I pulled it off without screaming.

"Let me see what I can do." The woman swiped my card through and handed it back across the counter as she kept her eyes on her computer screen. When she looked back up, I knew the news wasn't good.

"The credit card was denied," she said carefully, keeping her tone low enough that the people around us couldn't hear. Her chocolate brown eyes met mine, and her smile was warm as she looked across the desk at me. "Go right ahead and swear, darling. You look like you've had a rough day."

Tears stung hot at the backs of my eyes. I didn't realize one had escaped until she handed me a tissue, passing it across the counter without a word. I dabbed at my eyes, focusing on her name tag. "Thank you, Caroline."

"You're most welcome. I'm guessing you didn't know your credit card was maxed out."

I straightened my shoulders and shook my head with the ghost of a bitter smile twisting my lips. "Most definitely not. It was my fucking asshole of an ex-boyfriend."

"Well, I suppose the upside is he's your past, not your future," Caroline said.

"Oh, he's the past, all right. I guess I should get out of the line. I'm sorry for taking extra time," I muttered, managing a shaky breath.

"You're just fine. We can stand here and talk until you calm down. The world is not going to end if people need to wait a few minutes. There are two other lines," Caroline said matter-of-factly.

"Thank you," I whispered, sniffling after I took a deeper breath. This time I got enough air into my lungs to soothe my jangled nerves.

I carefully blew my nose. Without me asking, Caroline passed over another tissue and lifted a small wastebasket from under the counter. I tossed in the used tissue and straightened my shoulders in between several slow breaths. She tucked the wastebasket back under the counter and tapped her keyboard as if she was doing something. I knew she was simply giving me a few minutes to pull it together. I resisted the urge to apologize again. Her small kindness was a balm to my rattled state.

"New Orleans is a nice place," Caroline said softly. "There could be worse places to be stuck. Get your bearings and figure out what you need to do. I don't know you well, but you seem like a nice woman. Any man that would do this to you is an idiot."

"Most definitely," I replied.

Caroline tapped a few keys on her keyboard, giving me another moment. This brief interaction helped me brace myself.

"Thank you. I needed this," I finally said.

"Just make sure to take care of yourself," she said as I turned away.

I balled the soft tissue in one hand as I wheeled my broken suitcase behind me. It occurred to me that Caroline, a complete stranger, was the second person in the last few days to refer to Brett as an idiot. He sure as hell was. I supposed the only upside to this fiasco was at least now I knew he wasn't worth my time.

I wished I'd had a clear picture of who he was before I hopped on a plane to New Orleans. It had been three months since we'd even been intimate, and we'd managed only a few dates in that time. I was confused as to why he even wanted me to come on this trip. I wondered if he thought somehow my connection to Max would've perhaps smoothed some introductions for him.

Whatever. The second my thoughts turned to my brother, I realized he was probably my only parachute out of this situation—unless I intended to stay in New Orleans.

The only other alternative I could consider was applying for yet another credit card online and running up a bill to find somewhere to stay. Between blowing up all of my credit cards, Brett had also screwed me over on my lease in San Francisco. He'd known I was moving in two weeks and had contacted the landlord to tell her I'd changed my mind because we were moving in together. He'd finagled to get the deposit refunded to him.

The only reason he'd pulled that off was because months ago, he'd given me the name of his contact at the building, so he knew precisely who to call and bullshit. In the last few days of frantic phone calls since Brett had disappeared, I'd spoken to the property manager. She'd been horrified to learn Brett didn't have any claim to my deposit. That didn't change the fact that my money was still gone. I knew I had the option of taking legal action, but nothing would happen fast enough to help me now.

No matter what, I had to make a quick decision. Of course, I didn't need to do something impulsive, especially involving money.

With my polite face firmly in place, I stepped

back out into the sweltering heat and promptly collided with someone. "Oh! I'm so sorry," I said as my eyes swung up.

Before my gaze even made it to his face, I knew I had run straight into Nash Reynolds. What was it with me encountering him when my pride was so shredded? To be fair, the first time I met him, I'd sought him out.

Nash's eyes swept over my face. "What brings you back out of the airport, Mari?" he asked, his tone measured.

Considering that he already knew the outlines of what an idiot Brett was, I figured I might as well not bother being polite. "Apparently, Brett got us refundable tickets. He canceled mine to get the refund," I explained, my tone sharp.

Nash's eyes held mine, and I silently sighed. "Clearly, I wasn't aware of just what an ass he was. To give me a little credit, we haven't had sex in three months."

The moment that detail slipped out, I wanted to stuff the words back in my mouth. I had the worst habit of blurting things out when I was flustered.

Nash arched a brow. "Well, thank you for the information."

I laughed bitterly. "You're most welcome."

"How can I help?" he asked, his tone solemn.

Chapter Five

NASH

Mari looked tired, a sense of unease and weariness clinging to her. I found myself wanting to scoop her up and take her away—anywhere where she could relax and forget about all this. No one deserved to be taken advantage of, but the sense of protectiveness she elicited was unusual for me.

With my energy focused on work, I studiously avoided getting caught up in messy emotional entanglements. Yet, I found myself wanting to do whatever was necessary to hold Brett accountable and to tidy up whatever mess he'd created for Mari, which made no sense. I mentally shied away from contemplating just what I was doing and why.

Mari sighed again. "I don't know. I have no way to get home, and Brett seems to have maxed out every single credit card I have. Before you go thinking I was too trusting, they weren't even in his name. I'm pretty sure he figured out all my logins and..." Her words petered out, and she lifted a hand to brush a loose lock of hair away from her face.

I was torn between two impulses. On the one hand, I could simply buy her a plane ticket. On the other hand, I knew when she got home, she was going to find out the situation with her apartment if she hadn't already. I'd had a friend who happened to be a private investigator do a quick check on her. Among other things, he'd scouted up that she'd recently moved out of one place and had leased another. Except the lease had been terminated two days ago after Mari had arrived here in New Orleans.

I wanted a little time with Mari. She got to me. I wasn't thinking rationally, and I didn't care. I shook my thoughts loose and repeated my question. "How can I help?"

"Honestly, I should probably just stay here until I figure out a plan. I already know from talking to my landlord that I have to find a new place." Her mouth twisted in a bitter smile, although she didn't add more to that explanation. Ah-ha. So she did know. Well, at least I wasn't the bearer of that news. "No sense in paying for a plane ticket when I could use the money in other ways," she finished.

Because it was my nature, I got practical. "Do you need to go back for work?"

Mari shook her head. "No. My job's mobile. Not that it's the most lucrative, but I'm a journalist."

"Hmm. I recall Max mentioning that."

"Do you know my brother well?"

"Our connections are business, but I trust him and consider him a friend."

Mari lifted a hand and swiped away a bead of sweat rolling down her temple.

"I'd offer to buy your plane ticket, but I'm not sure that's what you want. Why don't we get out of this heat?"

Mari held my gaze for several moments, something flickering in the depths of her eyes. After a beat, she looked away, staring blankly into the rows of cars parked beyond the entrance to the airport. When she looked back, the only word I could think of to describe her was resigned. "Let's definitely get out of the heat."

"Come on." I reached for her suitcase, and she yanked it out of the way.

"I can get it," she snapped.

I eyed her for a second and then shrugged. "Mari, I would offer to help anyone with their luggage. It's just manners."

Her low laugh was like a light lash of the whip on the lust driving me ever since I laid eyes on her the other day. Although she was frazzled and frustrated and slightly wilting in the New Orleans heat, she was still breathtaking.

She was quiet as we walked. I flicked through the memory banks in my brain, trying to recall what Max had told me about his younger sister. He spoke fondly of her, and her mentioning she was a journalist had jogged my memory on that detail. I knew Max would be curious to learn what Brett had done. It wasn't the money so much. Given how much money Max had, he could easily remedy that situation. But, he wouldn't stand for the way Brett did this to Mari.

The air cooled as we walked into the parking garage. My hand rested reflexively on Mari's back and coaxed her in the direction of my car. The subtle touch was a habit, yet I had to admit I liked being able to touch Mari. I could feel the heat of her skin sifting through the thin fabric of her cream-colored blouse.

Being born and raised in New Orleans, my manners had been drilled into me by my mama. She always said manners were like butter—that they made every moment a little bit better just the way butter made food better.

"Right here," I said, coming to a stop at the back of my vehicle.

Mari's eyes swung to mine. "I suppose I might have expected something more ostentatious from you, Nash," she commented as she eyed my sleek black sedan.

I glanced down as I hit the key fob, and the

trunk popped open. "I might have plenty of money, darling, but I am at heart a very practical man. I also wasn't raised rich. This car is reliable as hell, and that's all that matters."

"No?" Mari queried as I took her suitcase from her and put it in the trunk.

"My daddy was a shrimper. He made decent money, but it's hard work. He always says a car is just something to get you somewhere."

Rounding to the passenger side, I held the door for Mari. I didn't miss the glimpse of her tan thighs when her skirt slid up as she sat down.

I could practically feel the wheels spinning in Mari's brain as I drove away from the airport. Considering that I knew she was in a bit of a financial bind, and I knew she had nothing more than a temporary place to stay if she went home, I offered up the easiest thing.

"If you looked me up, you probably know I own a number of properties in and around New Orleans. You're welcome to stay in one of the staff apartments at my main office building." I came to a stop at a stop sign and glanced sideways when Mari stayed silent. Her cheeks were pink, and she was staring out the window. It felt as if she were purposefully not looking in my direction.

After a moment, I prompted, "Mari?"

She turned quickly, her blue eyes colliding with mine. "Thanks for the offer, but I'll figure something out, Nash. I'm going to call my boss and see if there are any stories I can work on while I'm here."

A horn honked behind us, and I looked back at the road, turning and heading toward downtown. "Mari, it might seem like an extravagant offer, but it's really not. At any given point, I have several empty places available. It's honestly no trouble for you to stay in one. Plus, since I know your brother, I wouldn't feel right leaving you without somewhere to stay."

I kept my eyes on the road. I thought perhaps if I gave her the privacy afforded by indirect conversation, she might be less defensive about the situation.

After several more quiet beats, she replied, "Okay. I do appreciate it. I just need a few days to get my bearings and figure out what my plans will be."

"Excellent. Shall I go ahead and drive you there?"

Mari laughed softly, and I took that as a sign she was relaxing somewhat. "Seeing as I don't know where to go, I'm entirely reliant on you to tell me where it is."

When I took an exit leading to downtown New Orleans, Mari commented, "It sure is beautiful here. I'm glad I finally got to visit even if it wasn't the best vacation."

I slid my gaze sideways briefly and saw that she had unlaced her fingers over her knees, and her hands were relaxed in her lap now. "New Orleans is a wonderful city. Everyone should visit. I'm sorry you didn't have a good trip. Perhaps we can remedy that. Where were you supposed to stay?"

"I spent three nights at Creek's End Inn. It's …"

"Oh, I know right where that is. Gorgeous place. I know the Grantham family and am friends with Hannah. She's good people."

"Of course you know them," Mari said dryly.

"Of course?" I countered.

"You strike me as the kind of man who has connections everywhere. You know my brother, you know the Grantham family, is there anyone you don't know?"

"That's your brother and one family," I said as I shook my head. "Forgive me for being well-connected in the area where I live. As for knowing your brother, we have business connections. Because of my real estate business, I'm constantly in need of security. I'd think you know that's one of his specialties."

Mari looked my way with a slight smile. "I get it. I was just teasing." After a pause, she added, "Here's hoping I can enjoy my next few days in New Orleans."

"Let's make a deal."

"A deal?"

"Yes, a deal. I was born and raised here. Let me show you the city I love. She's a good friend."

"She?"

I lifted a shoulder in a slight shrug. "Yes, she." I forged ahead with my question. "Look, I don't know much about the nature of your relationship with your ex. He *is* your ex, right?"

"Oh, most definitely," Mari said firmly.

"I don't know what you intended to do on this trip with him, but he left, and he was pretty shitty about it if you ask me. I normally wouldn't comment on this, but since you told me, I might as well point out that it doesn't sound like things were all that great with y'all for the last few months. Consider this an entirely fresh start. Leave Brett in the dust and enjoy yourself here in Louisiana."

Exiting off the highway, I slowed when I came to a stoplight and glanced in Mari's direction. She was studying me, her gaze thoughtful.

After a moment, she let out a soft sigh. "I always thought of New Orleans as such a romantic city. Obviously, I know better now, but I thought maybe Brett and I could get things back on track this weekend. Don't go thinking I want him back. I don't. But it's just...Well, you said it best. He was shitty to me."

"You can still have a romantic vacation here."

I might've lost my mind, but I suddenly became bound and determined to make this trip far more than Mari expected.

Her cheeks flushed as she stared back at me. Just

when I thought she wasn't going to say anything, she did. "Okay then. Show me New Orleans."

———

"So, that's your tour," I said.

I looked across the room at Mari, where she was standing by the windows, which looked out toward the harbor. The Port of New Orleans was visible in the distance. With this building located a few blocks outside of the French Quarter, it was a mix of offices on the lower floors with my company occupying the entire second floor, and residential condos on the two upper floors.

As we'd walked around the small condo, Mari twisted her hair up into a knot and tied it. I was marveling at the fact that it was long enough to stay in place. Mari turned and crossed the room toward me, her footsteps echoing on the hardwood floors. She stopped beside me where I stood by the kitchen island that served as a divider between the small kitchen and the open style living room.

"Thank you, Nash. Now that I'm here, I can't tell you how much I appreciate this. I really won't stay long, but it'll give me a few days to pull some kind of plan together."

Having her stand this close revved my body's engine. She was so damn beautiful. She also smelled a bit like flowers, the scent drifting up and winding around me. My body tightened in reaction as I looked down into her eyes.

I forced myself to try to think clearly. "Like I said, it's no problem. I'm sure you can tell this place is empty." I gestured with my hand toward the space. While it was furnished, it was sparsely decorated.

Mari followed the arc of my motion before her eyes came back to me. "I can see that." Her mouth curled at one corner with a half-smile.

I was relieved to see some of the tension easing away from her finally. As we stood there, it distantly occurred to me that I usually had more capacity to set the tone of an interaction. I didn't know exactly what it was about Mari, but my physical reaction to her was so elemental and so powerful that it knocked me off my game slightly.

Right about now, I should've been making my exit. I had meetings and business to attend to. Lydia had already sent me about ten texts since I should have already returned to the office. As I stood there, I felt my phone vibrate in my pocket again and presumed it was Lydia reminding me of yet another thing I was probably running late for.

Yet, my eyes stayed on Mari, following the delicate line of her brow, down to trace over the clean angle of her cheekbone to her lush, oh-so-tempting lips.

I wanted to kiss her, something fierce.

I didn't realize I'd taken a step and closed the distance between us until I heard the soft hitch of Mari's breath in her throat and saw the blue of her eyes darken with desire. My heart was thumping a rough, wild beat inside my chest.

Just as I hadn't been thinking when I stepped closer to her, I was almost surprised to feel her soft skin under my fingertips when it landed along the side of her neck. I traced my thumb along her jaw-line, pausing when I reached her mouth, right below that dimple in the center of her bottom lip.

Chapter Six

MARI

I stared into the darkening swirl of color in Nash's eyes and tried to catch a breath. It felt as if all the air had been sucked out of the space around us. I was hot all over with my skin tingling and my pulse skittering off into a mad dash.

I wanted, no *needed*, to feel his mouth on mine. I'd never wanted to kiss anyone so desperately in my life. On the heels of barely a breath, I whispered, "Kiss me."

Although I had absolutely no doubt that Nash was a dominating and alpha man, in this moment, he demonstrated he had no trouble taking orders.

"Yes, ma'am," he murmured in that sexy drawl of his.

He stepped a fraction closer, and I felt the intense power and strength of him come against me. It was like walking into an electrified wall. Sensation jolted me and raced through me in hot ripples.

Everything felt slow and fast at once. Nash's hand slid around to cup my neck, and the feel of his palm dragging gently across my skin nearly made me moan aloud. He dipped toward me, and I arched into him, straining to meet him because I needed his touch.

With my heartbeat echoing through my body, his lips brushed across mine, sending tingles spinning through me. His lips were warm and soft. He didn't rush, and I didn't know if that was better or worse.

Considering that I was about to literally melt at his feet, it was a good thing he slid his arm around my waist and held me against him. When I felt the heat of his arousal, thick and hard against my belly, there was a gush of slick heat at my core, and I moaned against his lips.

He murmured something into our kiss. I couldn't decipher the words, but I felt them—endearing and dirty at once. When I arched closer, his tongue slipped into my mouth, sliding sensually against mine as I threw myself into the kiss. I felt wild inside and savored the way he set the pace. His fingers slid through my hair, as he devoured my mouth in a slow, sensual tease before drawing back and diving in again.

I lost all sense of where we were until I felt the vibration of his phone against the edge of my hip. It didn't stop. Nash gentled our kiss and lifted his head, catching my bottom lip lightly in his teeth before releasing it.

For an intensely charged moment, we simply stared at each other. Blood rushed through my ears, and my breath came in short pants. I could feel the rapid thud of his heartbeat while mine was banging against my ribs. I took a tiny bit of comfort in knowing that perhaps I affected him as powerfully as he affected me.

His phone began buzzing again. "I think you'd better get that," I said reluctantly.

His mouth twisted to the side, and he let out a soft sigh. "I should."

He stepped back, and I instantly missed his warmth and strength.

———

After Nash left to attend a business meeting, I took a few minutes to explore my temporary lodgings. The staff condo, as Nash described it, was on the top floor of the same building where his offices were located. Apparently, he owned the entire building. The condo offered a view of downtown New Orleans with the Mississippi River in the distance.

There was an open style living room and kitchen area with a tall ceiling and windows letting in lots of light. Dark hardwood flooring was a contrast to the cream-colored walls and the neutral colored furniture. A small oval kitchen island served as a dining area as well as a natural divider between the living room and kitchen. There was a round table beside the windows.

Beyond that main open area was a small entryway, and two bedrooms along with a bathroom. I certainly didn't need both bedrooms. The wiry thread of tension I'd felt ever since I'd woken and discovered Brett gone several days ago had finally started to ease in my shoulders. At least I had somewhere to be for a few days while I came up with some kind of plan.

The moment I thought of Brett and my overall situation, restlessness nudged me. I walked into the larger of the two bedrooms where Nash had carried my suitcase and began to unpack. Maybe I would only be here for a few days, but I wanted to be comfortable.

In the back of my mind, I considered calling my brother Max. He was due back from his trip with Harlow today. It didn't surprise me that he and Nash knew each other. Max knew a lot of people all over the country, most of them wealthy. Although my brother was quite wealthy, he was a good man and down to earth. We'd grown up solidly in the middle class in Pennsylvania. Our mother was now a retired teacher, and our father still ran his small mechanic garage right beside our parents' house.

Max was brilliant, and money seemed to just happen for him. Fortunately, he had his feet firmly on the ground. If they hadn't been before, they were even more so ever since he'd fallen in love with Harlow May, a hotshot firefighter from Alaska.

I adored Harlow and Max's story. They met entirely by chance when Max attended a wedding of one of his good friends from MIT who'd moved his business to Alaska. At the wedding, Harlow had been one of the bridesmaids for her close friend. Max was smitten with Harlow from the moment he met her.

Now, Max went back and forth between his company's headquarters in San Francisco and Alaska. It didn't really matter where he lived since he could conduct most of his business online. Max was the one who seemed blessed financially—it was like money just walked up and climbed in his pocket. On the other hand, I wasn't so lucky that way. I landed in journalism—which didn't pay particularly well. In fact, most months I would go so far as to say it didn't pay much at all. Barely enough to squeak by.

Brett had quite literally left me in the worst straits possible when he ran up all my credit cards. Even if I managed to straighten that mess out, I knew it would affect my credit.

"Fuck my life," I muttered to myself as I scrolled through an email on my phone.

It was an email from Brett with the tickets for

this trip. I couldn't believe he'd gotten refundable tickets and canceled mine for the refund. Of course, since he screwed me over with my lease, I wouldn't have had anywhere to stay when I got back to San Francisco anyway. My lease had just ended at my other place, and I'd put my things in storage until I could move into the new place the week after we returned. I'd been staying at a friend's apartment for a few weeks while she was out of town for work.

Even though it made me nervous because Max could be overprotective and I knew he hadn't liked Brett, I figured I might as well go ahead and let him know what happened. I quickly typed out a text.

Just so you know, Brett and I are over. I'm in New Orleans for a bit. I hope you and Harlow had a great trip. xoxo

After I hit send, I decided to take a shower. I needed to wash the sticky heat away from me.

Chapter Seven

NASH

Lydia poked her head around the door. "Everything all set for Mari?" she asked when I gestured for her to come into my office.

"Yes. She's upstairs in one of the staff condos. Thank you for getting it cleaned so quickly."

Lydia smiled as she crossed the room and slipped into the chair across from my desk. "It was no trouble. I was due to call them anyway. Is Mari doing okay?"

"I think she'll land on her feet. From what I can gather, that idiot Brett ran up all her credit cards and left her in a bind."

"I hope you told her she could stay in the apartment as long as she needs. Does she intend to fly back home soon?"

I shrugged. "I don't know. Apparently, Brett purchased refundable tickets for this trip and canceled her return flight for the refund. I'm gonna do a little digging this afternoon to see what other bullshit he's been up to."

Lydia pursed her lips. "Mari seems quite nice. Not that she would deserve it even if she wasn't nice, but it makes his behavior all the worse."

I chuckled at the fierce expression on Lydia's face. "I agree with you on that. Don't worry, Mari can stay as long as she needs. As you know, I know her brother, so I plan to reach out to him as well. We'll find a way to make Brett pay."

Lydia arched a brow, angling her head to the side. "This isn't like you."

"What isn't like me?" I countered, even though I knew precisely what she was talking about.

"Going out of your way like this. I think you like Mariana Channing."

"I'm just helping her out," I said even though I knew Lydia was right. "I know Max well enough that it wouldn't do for me not to make sure she's taken care of while she's here."

Lydia's smile was polite, but I didn't miss the sly gleam in her eyes. "Of course. If you're so worried, perhaps you should let her brother know what happened."

I had a mini stare down with Lydia before I chuckled. "I was already planning on talking with Max."

My main office phone rang, and Lydia stood quickly. "I'll get that from my desk."

After she left my office, I pulled up the contacts on my phone. While Max was a friend and business acquaintance, we didn't communicate often, so I needed to find his contact information. I hadn't spoken to him since he had helped with some of the tech for the security on the buildings I managed in downtown New Orleans.

Just then, my personal phone rang. I spun it around on my desk to glance at the screen. As if Max could somehow read my mind from thousands of miles away, his name flashed on my screen.

"What the hell?" I murmured to myself right before I answered. "Hey, Max."

"Nash, I hope you don't mind me calling out of the blue."

"I never mind you calling, Max. You did a damn good job of setting up those systems for me. Oddly enough, I was considering calling you just now."

"I bet I can guess why. My sister is in New Orleans. Harlow and I just got back from a trip, and Mari texted a few minutes ago."

"Mari's the reason I was about to call you. Why don't you tell me what you know? I'll fill in the gaps. For starters, she's fine. I offered her one of our staff condos, and she's up there now." Max grumbled something. "Look," I added, "if you're pissed I didn't call sooner it's because I literally just got back to my office. I'm not so sure she'll appreciate me talking to you without checking with her first."

Max's sigh was heavy through the phone. "I'm sure she won't. Her fucking ex. I don't trust the guy, so I had one of our guys put a trace on his spending. I expected him to try to take advantage of Mari. My guy tells me he canceled her return ticket and left her high and dry there."

"Exactly. Brett's an asshole if you ask me."

Max was quiet for a few beats. "Agreed on that count. Although part of me wants to say you should've called me the second you knew she was there, if you had, Mari probably wouldn't have let you help her."

"Don't tell me you want me to keep it quiet that we spoke. I might not know Mari all that well, but I'm guessing that would piss her off good."

Max chuckled. "You read her right. Mari does not appreciate me having an opinion about her life, especially her love life. I'll call her and let her know we've been in touch. In the meantime, can you do me a favor?"

"Anything."

"Keep an eye on her. Let me know if she leaves because I'm not sure she'll let me know right away."

"You two aren't close?" I asked.

"Oh, we're close, but the kind of close a brother and a sister only a year apart are. We get along now after driving each other nuts when we were kids.

Mari gets touchy when I have too many opinions. I told her I didn't trust Brett after the first time I met him. She wasn't too pleased with me. Harlow tells me I need to learn to keep my mouth shut."

I laughed. "I have a younger sister. I know how that goes."

"Did Mari happen to mention how long she plans to stay in New Orleans?" Max asked next.

"She's insisting she doesn't want to take advantage of me." Max couldn't see me, but I rolled my eyes hard at that. "She can stay as long as she likes."

"Good. Thanks for looking out for her, Nash. I'll be in touch."

After I hung up the phone, I took a breath, letting it out slowly as I leaned back in my chair and spun around to look out the windows. I'd have helped Max out no matter the circumstances, but I knew he wouldn't appreciate it if he knew I'd kissed his little sister.

I didn't even know what to think of that kiss. Mari lit a fire inside of me, and I wanted a chance to have more than a kiss with her. I was already restless to ask her out for dinner tonight.

Considering Max, I figured I'd better leave her to her own devices. I predicted she would be pissed at him, but I was relieved he'd initiated the call rather than me. Although I wouldn't hesitate to tell her I was equally concerned. I had a bad feeling about Brett. For better or worse, I intended to make sure he at least paid a financial price for trying to fuck her over.

Spinning away from the windows, I tapped my phone, pulling up a local guy we used to chase down financials when we were assessing properties.

"Trent here," he said, talking fast for a Southern man.

"Hey, Trent, it's Nash Reynolds. How're you doing?"

"Busy, busy. Yourself?"

"Same. I need to hire you for a not so typical job."

"You know I'll say yes. I love a change of pace."

"Here's the situation. A personal friend got screwed over by an ex. He maxed out all of her credit cards, although they were all in her name. I'd like you to do a forensic breakdown to see just how far it went and see if you can chase down any accounts connected to him."

"You got it. I do this kind of shit all the time, but not usually for you. What gives?"

"Doing a favor for a friend. I don't know if she'll ever get her money back, but I'd like to make things uncomfortable for him. While we're on the topic, you wouldn't happen to know if there's a way to slap charges on things like this, would you?"

Trent chuckled. "There's always a way, but if they were shared accounts, it gets a lot more difficult. Best way to deal with it is for the person affected to file fraud claims on every card. If it's enough money, they might get somewhere. If you willingly hand over or share an account, there's not a whole lot to do about this kind of fraud. Is this a nasty divorce? Those are usually when I get called for things like this."

"Nasty break up, but not a divorce. I don't even know if it was that ugly. He just ran her credit cards up and took off. At least, that's all I know for now."

"Damn, people can sure be shitty. Unfortunately for me, that's what pays my bills. Get me the deets, and I'll chase it down as far as I can."

"All right. I'll give you a call later. I want to run this by my friend before I hand over all the info."

Chapter Eight

MARI

"What the hell, Max?"

"I knew you'd be pissed, Mari. For what it's worth, I should apologize for telling you I thought Brett was an asshole the first time I met him. Even if he proved my point for me, I shouldn't have done that."

I wanted to throw the phone across the room, but this was my brother, and I did love him after all. I paced back and forth in front of the windows. "Oh yeah, Brett proved you right and then some."

"I also spoke to Nash Reynolds."

I could practically hear the trepidation in Max's voice. "Nash called you?" I sputtered.

"No, I called him. If you're gonna be pissed, be pissed at me. I know Nash because he hired me to set up the security systems on the buildings he manages in New Orleans. He's a good man. I wanted to ask him to check in with you in case you needed any help. Sounds like he beat me to the punch on that one."

I wanted to scream, but I bit my tongue. Hard. "Yes, Nash has been very helpful. I went to meet him when I realized Brett was gone. Brett left a note in his online calendar about meeting with Nash. Nash was dropping somebody off at the airport when I discovered Brett canceled my ticket for the refund."

"Don't be pissed at Nash. Be mad at me for being an overbearing older brother. Meanwhile, I'm gonna see if I can find Brett."

"I don't want to find Brett. I just don't want my credit all messed up."

Max said something in a mumble.

"What?"

Max's voice came back to full volume. "Well, if—" After an abrupt pause, Max began again, "That's Harlow telling me not to be an ass. Would you like to talk with her?"

"Please."

About the only woman Max didn't try to boss around was his wife. Harlow was a total badass and a hotshot firefighter to boot. She could handle herself and Max.

"Hey, Mari," Harlow's voice came through the line.

"Hey, Harlow. Max is being a big brother. Could you just tell him he was right about Brett? Now I know, and he can let that go."

Harlow laughed. "I can tell him, but you know your brother. It's all I can do to get him to back off with me sometimes."

"I feel like such an idiot, Harlow. Don't you dare tell Max this, but if I'm honest with myself, I tried to stay with Brett because I wanted to prove Max wrong. Instead, Brett turned out to be the over-achiever of assholes."

"Hey, don't beat yourself up. We all get to make mistakes with relationships. You know my history before Max. God, sometimes I can't even believe what an idiot I used to be."

"Oh, I can believe it. I'm feeling downright stupid now."

"Did you call your boss like you said?" she asked, referring to a text I'd sent earlier after she texted to check on me.

"I did. I'm all set. He's going to give me a few assignments in this area. It'll pay the bills while I figure out what to do next. Plus, Nash has promised to show me New Orleans the right way."

"Oh, really?" Harlow asked. "I've met Nash. He's pretty easy on the eyes."

The memory of the feel of Nash's lips over mine sent a wash of heat through me. He was more than easy on the eyes, but I wasn't about to get into that with Harlow.

"He's easy on the eyes, all right. I think he's just a Southern gentleman. I'll take it, because I'd like to see the city and not have my only memory be my asshole ex taking off and leaving me behind at a bed and breakfast."

"That'll be fun," Harlow replied. "Just forget about Brett. Don't let it get to you that Max didn't like him when he first met him. Max isn't likely to like any guy who's with you at first. He can't be considered objective."

"Well, that won't be a problem. I don't intend to date ever again. My luck sucks, and I think I'll stay single."

Although I couldn't see Harlow, I could imagine her eye roll. Gracious friend and sister-in-law that she was, she simply said, "Perfect then. You don't need to worry about it."

My phone chimed, indicating a text was coming through. Putting Harlow on speaker, I pulled the phone away from my ear and glanced at the screen. Nash's name was flashing. "Hey, I've got to go. Will you tell Max I love him?"

"Absolutely. Enjoy yourself."

I ended the call with Harlow and tapped the message window.

Checking to see if you need anything.

I ignored the shaft of disappointment. I didn't know what I expected, so I nudged aside the feeling.

All set. Thanks for checking.

There. I could be normal and brief too.

I crossed the kitchen and checked through the cabinets to discover that, while there wasn't much food, there were some basics such as coffee, tea, and crackers. I quickly made myself a pot of coffee. I made a mental note to pick up some creamer when I went to the grocery store.

I needed some food to tide me over for the next few days. I logged onto my email to check if I had received my assignment. My boss's promised email was already waiting. Tyson asked me to do a spread on small inns in the New Orleans area. Unfortunately, he thought I was still staying at Creek's End Inn and wanted that to be my starting place. I bit back a sigh. This meant calling Hannah.

I quickly replied to his email and told him I would get started. He didn't need to know the mess of my personal life. I figured perhaps I could persuade Nash to show me all the best places. He *had* offered to give me a proper tour of New Orleans.

I logged in to my bank online next to see just how much cash I might be able to withdraw for some groceries. Fortunately, my boss was going to send me a check in advance for gas money and lodging. Maybe I could use that to repay Hannah and stay here in the meantime.

When I logged into my online account, I was pleased to see my boss had already sent through a direct deposit in advance. It was only one thousand dollars, but I could buy some groceries and probably pay Hannah with that. While I was scanning the bank window, another deposit showed up in the account.

When I clicked on it, I narrowed my eyes. "Oh, for fuck's sake, Max." My overbearing brother wasn't above sending money over. It wasn't that I minded it, but I wanted to not be in my current situation and need the money.

While I contemplated sending Max a text, my phone chimed on the kitchen island counter where I was sitting on one of the stools. Spinning it around, I saw a text from Max.

I'm sure you're swearing at me. Let me help you out. It's not your fault you're in this situation, and Brett's an asshole. I'll track him down, and you can pay me back later if you insist. Love you.

I took a sip of my coffee and sighed as I stared at Max's text. I loved my brother, I really did. I was so happy he'd found Harlow because it has softened the sharp edges of him. After he'd been burned by his girlfriend in college, he'd gotten cynical. Finding Harlow had gotten him past his cynicism. He was kinder and gentler, even if he could still drive me crazy.

Lifting my phone, I quickly tapped out my reply. *I WILL pay you back. Love you.*

After hitting send, I looked up the closest grocery store and was pleased to discover it was within walking distance. I certainly didn't need to waste money eating out all the time. I changed into more comfortable clothes and good walking shoes.

Throwing my purse over my shoulder, I headed out. With it being late afternoon now, the humidity had broken and the air was slightly cooler. I walked along the sidewalk, glancing around at the lovely old homes. The famed balconies of New Orleans were in abundance with flowers spilling over the railings. Many of the people I walked by cast me a smile. The tension bundled in my neck and shoulders began to ease for the first time in days. Now that I had adjusted to the bitter reality of my relationship, or lack thereof, with Brett, hindsight was giving me a clear-eyed view. Although I didn't like how it happened, I was relieved it was over.

Brett had blown into my life with plenty of charm and good looks to butter me up during a fundraiser at an art gallery in San Francisco. Max was the reason I was there. He and Harlow were there because she was supporting a friend of hers from Alaska who sold whimsical painted furniture. Looking back now, I could see Brett probably saw me as his avenue to Max from that very night be cause I'd been standing with Max and Harlow when we first met.

My mind was nudged off of Brett when an older man with weathered skin cast me a broad smile as I walked by. I reminded myself I didn't need to dwell on Brett. I could be angry, but I was in New Orleans, and I intended to enjoy it.

Another block later, I saw the sign for the grocery store up ahead. It wasn't a large box type store, but a smaller neighborhood store. "Food and sundries" was all the sign said in curly blue script.

As soon as I stepped through the doors, the air was strikingly cool against my skin. There was hot, and then there was what New Orleans was. At its peak earlier when I was leaving the airport, the sun felt merciless, almost as if it was trying to melt me on the spot. Even now though, hours later, as the sun slid slowly down the sky, I couldn't imagine life here without air-conditioning.

I snagged a basket by the door and paused to survey the store and get a lay of the land. Grocery stores were a funny thing. They all had their own sense of organization. This one was filled with colorful produce in the front and cute little signs marking staff favorites as I meandered the aisles.

"Mari, hey there."

The moment I heard my name in Nash's voice, a prickle of awareness ran down my spine. I didn't know what it was about the way he said my name, but it felt special. Maybe it was the way the vowels rolled slowly off his tongue? Whatever it was, I reacted physically every time he spoke.

Turning in the direction of his voice, I found Nash approaching me. The man never seemed to be in a hurry, and now was no exception. He strolled toward me with his smooth gait. Even in the harsh fluorescent lighting of this grocery store, Nash managed to look kissed by the sun. His sandy hair glinted with gold didn't dull. His hazel eyes stood out, crinkling at the corners with his smile when he stopped in front of me.

"Hi, Nash." My voice came out breathy, and I felt foolish.

I wanted to think after my pride smashing experience with Brett that I would be immune to the charms of men, at least for a little while. But Nash was heavy on charm—even when he didn't seem to be trying —and nature had been exceedingly generous with him in the looks department.

"Grocery shopping?" he queried as he glanced down into my basket.

"What else would I be doing in a grocery store?" I teased in return, feeling my cheeks heat slightly.

"Excellent question," he drawled as he lifted his eyes to mine again. "I was thinking about texting you to see if you wanted to start your tour tonight."

"How come you didn't?" I countered, feeling a grin tug at the corners of my mouth.

Oh my God. I was actually flirting with him.

Nash's lips kicked up at one corner, and he cocked his head to the side. "I wanted to give you the night to settle in."

"Good point."

He looked back into my grocery basket and shook his head slowly. "Darling, all you have in there are bananas, hummus, and crackers."

"What's wrong with bananas, hummus, and crackers?"

"Not a thing, but it's certainly not a meal. Those are all snacks. That does it. You've lost your privilege of a night to settle in. We're going out to dinner," he said firmly.

I laughed, feeling my blush deepen. Against all of my better judgment, I *really* wanted to go out to dinner with Nash.

"Let me get a few more things, and then you can take me to dinner. Where are you taking me?" I turned and began walking as Nash followed along leisurely. Without a word, he reached over and divested me of my grocery basket.

"I can carry that, you know?"

"Of course, I know that. But, I was raised with manners. I can actually feel my mother's disapproval even though she's not here."

"You're ridiculous."

The only reason I didn't push the point was I didn't have any sense at all that Nash looked at women as wilting flowers who couldn't take care of themselves. In his case, I sensed his chivalry was deeply instilled and almost a habit. He was also alpha as all hell.

"Tell me what kind of place you'd like to go to for dinner, and I'll pick the perfect one." He looped our conversation back to my question.

"Your favorite hole in the wall diner," I said promptly.

"Oh, you are a woman after my heart. Diner food is my favorite, and I'll make sure you have the best."

Chapter Nine

NASH

"Oh my god, this is so good," Mari said, actually moaning with her next bite.

Sweet hell. I had genuinely wanted to take Mari out to dinner. It was also true that the food here was incredible. However, I hadn't reckoned with getting a hard-on at just the experience of eating a meal with Mari.

She was vocal about her pleasure. My body was of the opinion she would be that vocal about other pleasures.

"How is it, dear?" Carrie asked when she stopped by our table, her round blue eyes twinkling as she looked between us.

Mari finished chewing and dabbed at her mouth before she set her napkin back in her lap. "It's delicious. Nash told me this was the best diner in the world, and I'm here to agree."

Carrie smiled widely, her cheeks plumping up. "Aw, that is so sweet of you. Nash spoils us and tells us our food is good all the time. Between you and me, he's a charmer, so you never know."

"In this case, he's not trying to charm you—this burger is amazing," Mari said, gesturing with her hands and holding them up as if in prayer.

Carrie cast another smile between us. "Well, that just makes my night. Do y'all need anything else?"

"I couldn't eat another bite," Mari said.

"I'm all set. Bring the check when you get a chance, please," I added.

"Already got it." Carrie slipped a receipt book out of her pocket and tore one off, setting it in the middle of the table.

Nothing was fancy here. They still handled everything by paper. Considering that amazing food was really all that mattered, I was glad they hadn't tried to fancy this place up. Carrie hurried off with a wink, and I reached for the check just as Mari did.

"Are we gonna argue over who's paying for dinner?" I teased, curling my hand over hers.

"We don't need to argue," she countered quickly. "Why don't we just split it?"

I moved swiftly, shimmying my hand under hers and snatching the check away. "I don't split checks, and I invited you for dinner."

"Oh my God," she muttered. "You are *such* a man."

"Considering that I am, in fact, a man, I'm not gonna take that as an insult."

Mari rolled her eyes at that but didn't argue the point further as I paid at the register and we walked out.

We stepped outside into the warm night, and I glanced down to Mari. "Shall we take a walk down Bourbon Street? It's only a block over."

"I'd love that."

"Come on then," I said, reflexively reaching for her hand. For just a beat, I sensed she was startled, but her fingers laced into mine, and she began walking alongside me. "We can stop and get a drink too."

She stopped on the sidewalk and peered up at me. "Thank you," she said simply.

"For dinner?"

"Well, yes, but more than that. For offering to show me New Orleans, for helping me out. I was looking forward to this trip, and I thought it was ruined. Now, I think it might be better than I expected to begin with."

"I aim to please, darling."

Mari rolled her eyes slightly as she smiled.

"Now, what's that for?" I teased good-naturedly as we began walking again.

"You and your endearments. Actually, I don't

think it's just you."

"Definitely not. It's a southern habit. Women are just as generous with endearments as men around these parts."

Downtown New Orleans was always busy in the evenings, but it was busiest on Bourbon Street. Music spilled out from the many bars lining the street with tables filled at various outdoor patios. Mari looked around while we walked, occasionally commenting on some of the buildings and laughing at the crowds.

"Do you have a favorite bar?" she asked.

"I don't hit the bars too much these days, but I do have a few old favorites. Right here," I said, releasing her hand to slide my arm around her waist as a cluster of college students rather drunkenly meandered down the sidewalk and almost bumped into us.

We stepped into Johnny's Bar, one of the smaller and cozier bars in this busy area. There was a crowd, but I knew the owner, and Johnny saw me from behind the bar. He waved us over and magically managed to get us two free barstools in the corner of the bar against the wall where it was a little quieter.

Once we were seated, I gestured across the glossy wooden bar. "Mari, this is Johnny. He's an old friend. And Johnny, this is Mari. She's visiting New Orleans for the week, and I promised her I'd make it a good trip."

Johnny cast a roguish grin toward Mari. "You'll have to let me know if he doesn't treat you right."

Mari smiled in return. "So far, so good. He took me to the best diner."

"And now he brought you to the best bar in the French Quarter. I know Nash'll order a scotch, but what'll you have?"

"How are your margaritas?" Mari asked.

"The best," Johnny said, waggling his bushy white eyebrows.

"I'll take one then."

"What's your preferred flavor? Regular, strawberry, or watermelon?" Johnny asked as he prepped my scotch and slid it across the bar.

"Ooh, I'll have to try the watermelon. I've never had a watermelon margarita."

"Coming right up." As he began to prep her drink, he asked, "So where did my boy take you?"

"The Good Dinner Diner. Best burger I've ever had."

Johnny cracked a grin as he handed over Mari's drink. "See now, Nash is a smart man. He didn't go fancy; he just picked the best place. You best be careful, he's a charmer." With a wink, Johnny turned away when someone called his name. Glancing back, he added, "Y'all enjoy those now. Let me know when you need another."

"Thanks, put them on my tab," I commented. I

might not get out often, but I'd had a tab here at Johnny's since college.

"You got it." He was immediately swept into prepping drink after drink for the customers crowding around the bar.

Mari took a swallow of her margarita. "Mmm, this is yummy."

"Just like where I took you to dinner, everything is damn good here."

Mari spun on her stool to look toward the small stage in the front. A jazz band was playing a mellow set. I couldn't help but watch when Mari lifted her drink to her mouth, her tongue darting out to lick the salt on the rim.

My body tightened with a jolt of need, and I felt the press of my cock against my zipper. Fuck me. The effect Mari had on me was testing my control.

We stayed at the bar for a while. Although my arousal wouldn't abate, it was nice to relax with Mari. Dating hadn't been a priority of mine for some time. I'd been too focused on growing my business, much to the chagrin of my parents.

Once I started to do well financially, I'd wanted to build on it. My family had gotten by when I was growing up, but it hadn't been easy. There were late-night whispered conversations that I overheard about shrimp seasons that didn't go well and my dad trying to find extra work.

I dated here and there but didn't want to use the

time for anything more because work had been my focus. With the way I was reacting to Mari, I was wondering whether it was more that no one had caught my attention. Distraction was far too weak of a word to describe Mari's effect on me. My body was on high alert around her. As the bar became filled with more and more people, and I crowded closer to her, I noticed every shift of her leg pressing against mine.

She had a few more margaritas while I eschewed any additional drinks and nursed my single scotch. I needed to escort her back to the condo and drive myself home after that.

"Are you ready to go?" she asked, the feel of her whisper in my ear sending another shot of blood to my groin, which was already aching.

"Darlin', I'm ready to go whenever you are. Just say the word."

"I say we go now. I'm not much for staying up late, so it's a miracle I'm not falling asleep right here," she said before she drained the last of her margarita.

Moments later, we stepped out of the bar. Although people were milling about the sidewalks and the sounds of the crowds filling the various bars along Bourbon Street were all around, the noise was muted out here. I curled my hand around Mari's and walked her back to the condo.

I gave myself a little lecture on the way there,

telling myself she'd had a few too many drinks, and reminding myself that she was the little sister of a friend and business partner. I also knew with certainty that if I was going to let things play out further with Mari, I wanted us both stone-cold sober.

When we crossed the street and turned onto the block where my office building was located, I looked ahead to see the silhouette of a man leaning against the building. That, in itself, wasn't anything unusual. However, awareness jolted me as we approached. I might have only met him once, but I knew it was Brett.

I felt the instant Mari recognized him. Her hand tightened incrementally inside mine before her footsteps slowed and then stopped.

"What the hell is he doing here?" she muttered under her breath before looking up at me. "That's—"

"Brett. I know. Has he tried to reach out to you?"

She shook her head, her glossy tousled curls swinging lightly around her shoulders. "No. I haven't gotten any unknown calls. The last time I tried his number, it wasn't in service. Ugh! I do *not* want to deal with him. We had a good night."

I loved that she said *we*, but now wasn't the time to dwell on that. "I don't see any way around it. Avoiding him will only prolong the inevitable. I'm with you. I sure as hell don't mind giving him a piece of my mind. Come on."

Mari held still on the sidewalk for a moment before she shrugged. "Fine. Let's get it over with."

She began tugging me along. Once she'd made up her mind to face him, she appeared to relish the opportunity. With her skirt swirling around her knees, the low heels of her sandals clicked on the sidewalk as she strode briskly toward Brett where he waited right outside the entrance to her building, or rather, my building.

I filed that little detail away. Unless he was tracking her, he shouldn't have known where she was. Mari stopped several feet away from him, keeping her fingers laced with mine as she rested her other hand on her hip.

"What the hell are you doing here, Brett?" she demanded.

I didn't miss Brett looking down at our joined hands and up to my face before he looked back at Mari. He affected a sheepish expression. "Hey, Mari. I'm glad I tracked you down. I'm sure you've been wondering where I was, but it's all a big misunderstanding."

"Misunderstanding?" Mari practically spat out. "Brett, you totally screwed me over. You left in the middle of the night, you broke my lease and stole my deposit, you left me with the bill at Creek's End Inn *and* ran up all of my fucking credit cards. That's not a misunderstanding."

Brett shifted on his feet, anger flashing in his

eyes. He looked toward me. "How do you know each other?"

I waited in simmering silence. Much as I wanted to grab Brett by the scruff of the shirt and slam him against the brick wall directly behind him, I sensed it was important for Mari to handle this, so I hung back.

Mari laughed, the bitter tension in her laughter twisting my heart slightly. She didn't deserve to be bitter, and it made me sick that an asshole like Brett had ever even had a shot with her.

"I'm sure you can figure it out. You were logged into your work calendar on my phone, so when I was trying to find you, I saw that you had noted a meeting with Nash here. Unlike you, he's a fucking gentleman."

"Wow," Brett said, rolling his eyes. "Already moving on. I thought you wanted last weekend to be our chance to reconnect."

"Oh my fucking God! You're such an asshole. Yeah, I said that I hoped we'd reconnect. Because we might as well have broken up months ago for all the time we've spent together. If I'd been aware of everything you were capable of, I certainly wouldn't have said it. Don't even try to fucking guilt trip me," Mari said with a hard glare.

Brett's gaze shifted between us as if he was trying to get a measure of the situation. I was pleased to discover my presence confused him enough he didn't know how to handle it.

"Look," he began, his tone placating. "I can see why you might be upset, but if you'll just give me a chance to explain—"

Mari shook her head sharply. "Shut up and leave me alone."

Anger flashed in Brett's eyes again. When he opened his mouth to speak, I shook my head. "You heard her," I warned. "Get the hell out of here."

"Fuck you both." With another muttered curse, Brett turned and stalked across the street. I was relieved there were still people milling about because it minimized the possibility of him making more of a scene.

I could feel a subtle tremor running through Mari where I held her hand. "Let's get inside," I murmured, releasing her hand to slide my palm down her back and coax her gently forward.

Inside, I confirmed with the security guy at the desk that all was locked down for the night already. I also made a mental note to call the main security center as soon as I left the building tonight to make sure they ran a full scan and confirmed everything was in working order. At least here, Mari was protected by one of her brother's high-end security systems. I knew I would need to alert Max about this development with Brett, but that would have to wait.

I'd meant what I said earlier and intended to give Mari her space tonight. Although there was no way I'd have turned down dinner with Mari, I'd been planning to use the time tonight to do some more research on Brett's situation. I knew his financials were poor because I had my usual report drawn up when he'd asked to meet, but I hadn't dug deeper because there'd been no point then. Since Brett had shown up to find Mari, there was both a reason to delve further and a sense of urgency behind it.

After the elevator took us to the top floor of the building where all the condos were, Mari glanced up at me as she keyed in the lock combination. "I don't want to think about this, but I can't figure out how Brett knew I was here."

I'd been hoping Mari wouldn't contemplate that detail. "Let's get inside," I commented as another couple stepped out of the elevator and began walking down the hall in our direction.

Mari quickly punched in the combination, and we stepped inside. She walked over to the windows, letting her purse slide off her shoulder and dropping it on the couch as she walked past it. I stopped at her side, and the magnetic pull to wrap her in my arms was strong. Between my awareness of her three margaritas and our very recent encounter with Brett, I didn't think that was a good move.

I stuffed my hands in my pockets and looked out

across the glittering skyline of New Orleans and the dark river in the distance beyond.

"Between your brother and me, we'll chase down what's going on with Brett. This building is completely secure. Not sure how he found out you were here, but I'm going to double-check with security. It's staffed twenty-four-seven already, and the building locks automatically after eight p.m."

I heard Mari's breath escape in a slow sigh when she turned to look up at me. "I feel like I'm turning out to be an awful lot of trouble for you, Nash."

"You're no trouble, none at all."

She looked away, out to the skyline again. My eyes traced the elegant arch of her brows and the angle of her cheekbone. They snagged on her plump lips, and the urge to kiss her was piercing and sharp.

When she looked back toward me, her brow was knitted with worry, and her eyes were troubled. "I feel like an idiot."

"You're not an idiot. There's nothing wrong with trusting someone. It's just that untrustworthy people take advantage of our trust. You already knew things weren't going well with Brett, but you gave him a chance. The way others treat us only tells us something about them. Brett's the asshole here. You're not an idiot. Let Max and I see what we can do. We'll make sure he can't keep screwing with your money."

Mari murmured something indecipherable under

her breath. I didn't realize I'd stepped closer until my eyes landed on the rapid flutter of her pulse in her neck. Her eyes met mine again. "I hate when I can't clean up my own messes."

"Someone taking advantage of you and screwing you over isn't your mess."

With Mari's bright blue gaze holding mine, I let my fingers trail through the ends of her silky dark curls. She had this way of snatching my thoughts from me. Perhaps, it was more that she wiped out my ability to think clearly.

Without a single conscious thought passing through my mind, I dipped my head and brushed my lips over hers.

Chapter Ten

MARI

The feel of Nash's lips on mine sent flames licking through my body. I sighed against his mouth and pressed closer. I craved the feel of his strength and warmth encompassing me. He murmured something against my lips, and I slipped my hand around his nape, my fingers teasing along the edge of his collar.

With a muttered imprecation, Nash's hand slid down my back, and his tongue swept inside my mouth as he angled his head to the side. In a matter of seconds, I was swept into our kiss—the sensual glide of his tongue against mine, the way he held me strong and sure in his grip.

Just as the fierce fire was pulling me in, Nash drew back swiftly. A moan of protest slipped out. I wanted to yank him back, but he broke away entirely and took a few steps away.

"Fuck," he muttered as he ran a hand roughly through his hair and stuffed the other in his pocket. Turning away, he stared out the windows for a moment. When he looked back toward me, his eyes were dark. "I promised myself I wasn't going to do that."

"Why?"

Argh! I hated how much I wanted to know. Why couldn't I play this cool and simply dismiss him?

"Because I respect you, and your brother—"

"Oh my God! Don't you dare tell me you mentioned our kiss before to Max."

Nash shook his head sharply. "If you'd let me finish my sentence, you would've heard that it's just that I respect your brother, and I don't think he would appreciate me doing this. Not now, not after what just happened to you."

"Max has no say in my sex life," I said, my voice coming out with a high pitch.

Nash eyed me with trepidation. "Mari, I'm not saying your brother should have a say in this. It's that, well, you just came out of a relationship. Max might think I'm taking advantage. Not to mention, I don't want to be your rebound."

Anger laced through me, tangling up with the tumult of desire still humming in my veins. "You're not a rebound," I murmured. "Like I told you, Brett and I were practically broken up." Again and again, I wondered why the hell I said yes when Brett called and asked me about this trip. Maybe it was my pride, maybe it was me wishing there was something more for me with anyone, and Brett happened to be convenient.

"That's not my point," Nash said.

We stared at each other, and the air felt charged around us. After a long moment, Nash took a step closer. "I didn't expect this, but whatever happens between us, I don't want you to think it's just a quick thing for me. I'll see you tomorrow. Let me take you to lunch or dinner."

"Shouldn't you be at work tomorrow?" I was being stubborn, and I knew it, but whatever.

"If I feel like taking time off, I will. See you tomorrow. I'll be in touch about when." At that, Nash bent low once more and brushed a brief kiss across my lips. It felt as if I'd literally been shocked as the electricity spun through my system when he stepped away.

"Good night, Mari," he said when he reached the door.

Flustered, hot, and frustrated, I simply nodded. I sensed the beat of hesitation in him, but he moved decisively after a moment. The door shut behind him, and I heard the lock automatically click.

As soon as Nash was out of my sight, doubts and recrimination began to crowd my thoughts. I felt so foolish. Here I was, craving Nash's attention and touch. I didn't doubt he was attracted to me, but I shouldn't have let myself read any more than that into it. He was right. Well, except for caring about my brother's opinion.

I loved Max, but it was my stubborn reaction to his dismissive opinion on Brett that probably contributed to me staying in that stupid relationship—if I could even call it that—longer than I should've. If I ever doubted whether Brett was using me, his recent actions had made that abundantly clear.

The moment my thoughts tripped over Brett, a sense of unease rippled through me, and my gut churned with anxiety. I didn't understand how he'd tracked me down here. I certainly didn't understand why he would think we could talk this through somehow.

If there was one piece of sanity in the midst of my emotional confusion, it was that I didn't trust Brett. I firmly knew I didn't want to revisit anything with him. We were over, and I should've recognized it sooner.

When I looked back on when he asked me about coming on this trip, I should never have agreed. He'd been distant and sporadically in touch for the last few months or more. I hadn't even particularly missed him. I thought perhaps it was just my own not-so-great self-esteem around relationships and the sting to my pride. As if those two things alone weren't enough, if I was honest with myself, it was my pride that drove me to prove Max wrong that really made a mess of it all

Love or not, that was a funny thing about brothers. You didn't want them to be right. Hell no.

Uncomfortably aware that Brett somehow knew I was in this building, I checked the security panel by the door before getting ready for bed. Once I'd taken care of washing my face and brushing my teeth, I laid down. I was comfortably propped up on the pillows and scrolling through my e-reader to find a book to read when my phone vibrated on the nightstand beside the bed. Lifting it, I saw a text from Nash.

I had the security team run a check on all the systems for the building. Everything is locked down. Don't forget there's a security guard there all night handling the door. If you need anything, don't hesitate to call him. I'm forwarding you his direct number. If anything happens, please call me.

Immediately following that text, Nash forwarded the number for the security guard. I set my phone back on the table and smiled slowly as a sense of warmth spun around my heart. I didn't know what to think about my response to Nash. He was going out of his way for me, and I truly did appreciate it. Lifting my phone again, I typed out a quick reply.

Thank you. I appreciate everything you're doing. See you tomorrow.

I was enjoying a cup of coffee with a bagel and some cream cheese while I researched local inns for my story. Considering I could now pay Hannah for my stay at Creek's End Inn, I needed to start there. Pulling up her contact information in my phone, I called.

"Good morning, Creek's End Inn."

I thought this was Hannah 's voice, but I wasn't one hundred percent sure. "Good morning. I'm hoping to speak with Hannah Grantham."

"You found her. This is Hannah. How can I help you?"

"Hi Hannah, it's Mari Channing."

"Oh, hey, Mari! So good to hear from you. How are you?"

"I'm doing much better than when we last spoke. I'd like to pay you for my stay. I'd also like to follow-up and see if I could stop by for a piece I'm doing on local inns in the area."

"You could stop by no matter what, but I would never turn down free publicity," Hannah replied. I could hear the smile in her voice, and it eased the thread of tension inside. Despite her graciousness about the situation, I'd been worried about the bill.

"Perfect. Seeing as I've already stayed there, I would give it nothing less than five stars. I'd love to chat about the history of the area and need to get a few photographs if that's all right."

Hannah and I chatted for a few more minutes, and I took care of the bill over her protestations. She only reluctantly agreed after I explained it just didn't feel right for me to let it slide.

"So, you'll be in the area for a while though?" she asked.

"At least for a week."

I explained my assignment, and she offered to give me a list of recommendations for other inns nearby. Because Hannah was by nature a generous person, I imagined she often recommended other places she respected. She didn't seem short on business and was one of the all-boats-lift-each-other types of people.

"Where are you staying while you're here? If you don't mind me asking."

"To make a long story short, I'm staying in one of the staff condos through Nash Reynolds. He knows my older brother through business."

"Oh, that's great. Nash is a nice guy. So easy on the eyes too," she teased. "Considering how much real estate he owns in New Orleans, I'm sure he's got plenty of options for you. Please do give Nash my best."

"Of course I will."

We firmed up when I would stop by for photographs. I got off the phone feeling a bit accomplished. It was just one story, but I felt like I was at least getting my equilibrium back. I might not know where I was going to land as far as where I lived, but I had a job that could travel with me, and I would sort out this mess created by Brett.

After I finished my call with Hannah, I reached out to a few other places from the email she sent with recommendations. I also spent a little time online doing some preliminary research on other inns. Lastly, I followed up and finalized my most recent assignment and sent it off to my editor.

I leaned back in the chair at the small round table off to the side of the kitchen with a satisfied sigh when I hit send on my last email. My life might have been turned upside down in some ways, but it felt good to get my bearings again.

When it came to my career, I'd kind of stumbled into my online journalism job. During college, I'd ended up working for one of the college newspapers mostly because I had a crush on a guy who worked there. He turned out to be an asshole—I seemed to have an excellent radar for assholes—but he left his job at the paper, and I stayed on. It wasn't great money, but it was enough for me to cover my bills and much more flexible than many other jobs. Although my brother was loaded now, back then, we were both scrambling just to get by.

After that, I'd gone on to get my graduate degree in journalism. It certainly wasn't the most lucrative field, but I enjoyed writing. My current job gave me a lot of flexibility. I could travel and had my pick of subject matters to explore for the most part—and when you add to that I had a supportive boss, it was a great fit. Maybe I was close to broke at the moment, and maybe I needed to figure out what the hell was next, but I had work. For the moment, I also had a place to stay.

The second I thought about just how temporary my living situation was, my mind spun onto dueling tracks of anxiety. I needed a plan because this wasn't a long-term prospect. There was plenty to worry about in that category. Then, there was Nash. It was *sooooo* not smart to be crushing on him. It didn't seem to matter if it was smart. My body and heart weren't getting the memo. I was *totally* crushing on him. Hard.

Merely thinking about our kiss had me leaping out of my chair and pacing restlessly in front of the windows. I didn't even know what to think of his misplaced chivalry. I definitely knew what I thought about him worrying about what my brother might think. For God's sake, Max had too many opinions about my love life. It stung a little bit. My pride had taken a big hit to the chin with Brett.

How the hell could Brett figure out where I was staying? That bothered me. A lot. I'd already changed my passwords on every single account I had. I just hoped he hadn't done something I couldn't find.

As if the universe was mocking me, my phone rang, the vibration on the table loud from where I was pacing back and forth in front of the windows. Striding back to the table, I glanced down at the screen. An unfamiliar number flashed there.

All worries about Brett aside, I never answered unknown calls. The deluge of robocalls, often masked, was exhausting and had trained me to be highly skeptical. Returning my phone to the table, I waited to see if whoever called left a message. Once the banner showed a voicemail, I hit play.

"Hey, babe. It's Brett. This is a temporary number. I don't know what the deal is with you and Nash Reynolds, but we need to talk. Call me as soon as you get this."

I almost hit delete before considering that perhaps I should save the message in case anything weird happened. Setting my phone back down on the table, I muttered, "I'm not your fucking babe."

There was no way in hell I was going to call Brett.

Chapter Eleven

NASH

"What did you find?" I asked Trent.

Trent leaned back in his chair, drumming his fingertips on the leather armrest as he regarded me. "You're not gonna like it."

Narrowing my eyes, I replied, "Just hit me."

"You already know all the financial info. He also opened four new credit cards in her name and applied for a business loan," Trent explained. Trent was a private investigator I'd known for years. Whenever I needed to dig deeper into something, I turned to him for help.

"Okay, none of that's all that unexpected given the situation. Anything else?"

"Yeah. Now you can add that he put a tracking chip on her phone. That's how he traced her to your building."

"What the fuck? Please tell me you already deactivated it."

"If I deactivate it, he'll know. Instead, I rerouted it to a burner phone I purchased. That phone is just going to sit with me during the day. I'll drop it off with your security in the evening at your office building. That's what we'll do until you're ready for us to cut bait."

I was pissed. As Max had guessed, Brett was unquestionably using Mari. Not that I'd been wondering about that detail. She didn't have a ton of money, in fact not very much at all, according to Max. As he put it, she stubbornly refused his help. Looking over at Trent, I shook my head slowly. "My best guess is he hopes to get investments through his connections with Mari. When he didn't get what he wanted, he decided to ruin her credit instead of his."

Trent nodded. "I can put a hold on everything he did money-wise under her name, but I need your clearance."

"I need to talk to Mari first."

This topic was dead last on the list of things I wanted to discuss with Mari. Brett was turning out to be more underhanded than I'd considered. For Mari's sake, I had wanted this to be a clean break for her. His actions were making that difficult.

I promised Mari a good week in New Orleans. This topic was decidedly *not* good. Concern kept pinging through me every time I considered Brett showing up last night.

"Let me know when you talk to her. All she needs to do is put a freeze on her credit, and that'll stop him in his tracks," Trent said.

"Yeah, I know," I said as I stood from my chair. "Thanks for your quick work, and I'll talk to her today. I don't want to delay on any of this."

Moments later, I stepped out, the heavy afternoon heat only serving to add to my frustration. Not that I didn't expect it, mind you. Louisiana was hot most of the time. My phone felt like it was burning a hole in my pocket. I wanted to call Max and run this by him before I talked to Mari, but I knew that would piss her off.

When I felt the vibration of my phone as I walked down the street, I slipped it out quickly and glanced down to see Hannah Grantham's name flash on the screen. I didn't hesitate to answer.

"Hey, Hannah, what can I do for you today?"

"Just calling to give you a small piece of my mind," she said tartly.

"Excuse me?"

"Look, Nash, you're a gentleman and my family has known yours for years. I know you're a good man, but I want to make sure you're not gonna do anything to hurt my friend, Mariana Channing."

"Well, uh, this is out of left field."

"Oh, don't start with the sports metaphors with

me just because my husband plays one professionally," she drawled. "Mari stayed at Creek's End Inn with her ex, who took off in the middle of the night. When I spoke to her, she mentioned you'd helped her out. You're a good man, but she does not need a fling. You're too charming for your own good."

I was relieved Hannah couldn't see me rolling my eyes. Although I wasn't too close to Hannah, I knew her socially. Her family went as far back in New Orleans as mine. I crossed paths with Hannah and her family with regularity, and of course, everyone knew who her basketball star husband was.

Although I hadn't expected such a call from Hannah, I appreciated her protectiveness of Mari.

"No need to worry, Hannah. I met Mari when she stopped by looking for her ex. I happen to know her brother because he handled security for my buildings. I offered Mari a place to stay. That's it." Obviously, I stayed silent on how much I wanted to kiss Mari again and then some.

"I'm glad I needn't worry. You keep being nice, you hear me?"

Although Hannah might be nosy, I knew I'd hear it if I harmed a single hair on Mari's head. Little did she know I liked Mari. Big time. "Of course. Didn't you just say I was a good man?"

Hannah laughed. "All right, all right. I'm glad you offered Mari a place to stay. She was pretty stressed out when she checked out of here."

"I can imagine. Anything else you need to lecture me on?

"No, but thank you for listening," Hannah countered smoothly.

After that call with Hannah, I wondered just what the hell I was thinking with Mari. Perhaps the issue was that I *wasn't* thinking. I certainly hadn't been looking for romance. Work occupied all of my time, and I knew Mari would probably consider me a rebound.

Yet, I was ignoring all of those contingencies. I wanted her.

When I reached my office building after returning from the short stroll from Trent's office, I welcomed the blast of cool air that hit me when I walked through the doors.

"Hey, Greg," I called, lifting my hand in a wave just as the security guy hung up the phone at his station, where he manned all the comings and goings in the building.

"Howdy, Nash," he replied.

Strolling over, I asked, "Schedule's all set for an extra guy during the nights?

"Of course, sir."

"How many times do I have to tell you not to "sir" me?"

Greg shrugged. "It's a habit. You're my boss."

"I hired you to manage security because I've known you since elementary school, Greg. It's damn strange when you call me sir. Now that we got an extra guy lined up for nights, I'd like to plan to keep that staffing level in place going forward."

"Not just while Miss Channing is here?" Greg asked in return.

I nodded. "That's right. She prompted it because of her situation, but I think it's good for the business and our tenants."

"Will do. I'll make it permanent on the schedule, and get going on making sure we have staff lined up. Anything else you need today?"

"Nope. Thanks for everything."

After I stopped by my office and caught up on everything Lydia had left in a list on my desk, I called Mari.

Chapter Twelve

MARI

I sighed as I set down my fork and looked across the table at Nash. "Oh my God. I think I could live off biscuits and gravy."

Nash's lips curled in a slow grin, and he winked. Butterflies took flight in my belly, spinning madly as heat prickled over the surface of my skin. Nash Reynolds was dangerous. Everything he did felt like a seduction. To make matters worse, I didn't think he was purposely trying to seduce me—at least not constantly.

"I know I could," he drawled before lifting his coffee cup and taking a swallow.

He had called me this morning from his office, announcing day two of my NOLA experience. This time, he took me to a diner on the outskirts of town. Gulls called, and a soft breeze gusted off the Gulf waters as we enjoyed breakfast out on the deck of this little diner. All they served was breakfast, and they closed at noon.

After Nash set his coffee cup down, he added, "I promised you a thorough NOLA experience. Biscuits and gravy are a big part of that."

"Well. Thank you. I doubt I would have found this place on my own."

"My pleasure." He dipped his chin in acknowledgment.

At the word pleasure, my pulse skittered wildly, and I could manage nothing more than a shallow little breath. "Do you need to get back to the office after this?" I asked, grasping for something to talk about, anything to get my mind off of thinking naughty thoughts about Nash.

"I'm yours for the rest of the day, darlin'. I did promise I'd give you the week."

Oh dear God. Every time he called me darlin', my toes curled, and my belly flipped. A little thrill also raced through me at the word promise. It was just words that were getting to me now. "Don't you need to go back to work?"

"That's the advantage of owning my own company. If I feel like moving things around, so I have time to spend with you and make sure you enjoy New Orleans, then that's what I'll do. This week, you're my priority."

"Oh." I snatched my coffee up and took a quick swallow.

Mentally trying to do anything to stop practically panting over Nash, my mind latched onto Brett. Thinking about Brett was sure to pour cold water on anything. "Brett left me a message this morning."

Nash's gaze sharpened immediately. "What did he say? Did you call him back?"

"Of course not. I certainly don't want to talk to him. I wanted to delete it, but considering the weirdness, I thought I should save it. Here."

I fished my phone out of my purse and tapped my screen to pull up the voicemail before handing it to Nash. He hit the speaker button, and Brett's message played again. Just the sound of Brett's voice grated on my nerves.

"I don't understand why he's calling. At all. He screwed me over big-time. Whatever. It's stressing me out that he knows where I'm staying."

Nash eyed me for a long moment before he nodded, almost as if to himself. "I need to tell you something. I have a friend who's a private investigator, top-notch. I asked him to do a little digging. Not only did Brett run up every credit card of yours, but he opened four accounts in your name."

Anger flashed hot inside. "What? Are you kidding me?"

"This is not the kind of thing I would kid about."

I shook my head and let out a shaky breath. "All right. I'm trying to wrap my brain around the fact you hired someone to dig into this behind my back, but thank you. Is there anything else I should know?"

Nash took a breath and rolled his shoulders. "Brett also applied for a business loan under your name and put a tracker on your phone. Don't worry; my friend rerouted it to a burner phone that he carries. He'll drop it off every evening with the security guard where you're staying. That way, it'll look like you're in the building where Brett expects you to be."

I felt sick, and my gut churned. I was suddenly hot and cold all over. Oh my God. I immediately pulled up my phone, swiping through the screens to see whatever Brett had put on there.

"You're not going to see it, Mari." Nash paused, studying me. His gaze felt as if it were boring into me, and I didn't like how vulnerable and unsettled I felt. "I haven't spoken to Max about this, but I think we should tell him today. My buddy's good at tracking things down because that's his job. But your brother has more tools at his disposal."

I took a deep breath, letting it out in a gust. "I know, I know." I took another sip of my coffee. "I'm guessing it wasn't easy for you to wait to call Max."

Despite my distress and anxiety around what the

hell Brett was doing, warmth curled around my heart at the knowledge that Nash didn't try to run roughshod over me and let Max know himself. I sensed that holding back wasn't easy for him.

"Hell no," Nash said bluntly. He paused, his gaze holding mine for a beat. He appeared to be considering his words carefully. "Of course, I wanted to call him right away. The only reason I didn't was because I like you."

"What?"

"Let me put it more directly. I want you. I want a chance with you. And no, it's not just about how much I want you. I want you. Badly. But I respect you, so I waited to ask you before I called Max."

"What if I want to call him first?" I retorted, flushing with an acute awareness at just how bluntly Nash told me what he wanted. Coming off of my shitty not-really-a relationship with Brett and feeling unwanted, I felt betwixt and between with how direct Nash was about his feelings toward me. I thought all he wanted was sex. I didn't even know what to think now.

Nash's eyes took on a gleam. He leaned across the table, resting one elbow on it. He curled his hand around mine where it sat on the table, his thumb brushing lightly across my knuckles and sending little licks of fire chasing over my skin and radiating outward.

"Well, darlin', then I would tell you to call him right now. Because I'm not waiting any longer."

I let out a startled laugh. "Now?"

"Yes. Now." He spun my phone on the table to face me again. "Put him on speaker."

My heart was drumming a fast beat in my chest, and Nash had me all flustered with the subtle brush of his thumb. I swallowed and looked away, relieved to escape from his probing eyes. Pulling up Max's number, I tapped to call.

Max answered immediately. "Hey, Mari. What's the update?"

"Nice to talk to you too, Max. Can we start with how are you?"

My brother didn't even bother to conceal his sigh. "How are you?"

"Well, I'm kind of freaking out, and you're on speakerphone. I'm here with Nash."

"Hey, Max," Nash chimed in.

"Glad you're there, Nash. What's the update?"

I rolled my eyes and leaned back in my chair, gesturing with my free hand toward Nash. He didn't let go of my other hand and slightly tightened the curl of his fingers around my palm.

Nash quickly summarized what he had shared with me a moment ago, ending with, "You may have already done this homework yourself. Any updates for us?"

Max's voice was tight when he spoke. "I chased

down the financials, but that's it. Mari, you need to put a freeze on your credit now."

"I will. I'll call as soon as we finish this."

"I wouldn't suggest calling. Go back to Nash's office and do it from there. Cell phones are notoriously insecure. Thank you for asking your guy to look into this, Nash. Mari, give us a few more days before you respond to Brett. I'd like to see if I can suss out why he's doing this. He's not particularly sophisticated, so I'm hoping it's just for money. In the meantime, please tell me you're gonna stay put. I trust the security at Nash's building."

I glared at the phone. I never appreciated my brother getting all high-handed with me. My irritation at this moment was layered. Regardless of my frustration, I felt frightened by what Brett was doing. He'd gone from being just an asshole who made me feel like a fool to someone who was committing real crimes. I didn't want to need anyone's help, but I did.

"Max, you don't need to get all bossy about it. I'll stay put. I don't like you trying to tell me what to do, but it's totally unnecessary since safety is more important than my pride. Nash has offered me a place to stay, and even if Brett knows where I am, I feel safe there."

I looked up and collided with Nash's waiting gaze. The look there sent my pulse off to the races.

He squeezed my hand, and the intensity held in his eyes stole my breath.

I didn't even hear half of what my brother started to say—but I quite clearly heard the irritation in his tone—and quickly yanked my eyes away from Nash's gaze to look down at the phone. "What?"

"Did you hear anything I just said?"

"No, the connection got a little staticky," I lied. When I dared a look at Nash, his lips curled in a sly, knowing grin. I wasn't about to fess up the connection had been totally fine, unless you counted the static in my brain created entirely by Nash and his sexy eyes.

"I said something to the effect of thank God you're being sensible," Max said.

"What Max means is he's glad you have a place to stay, and he's sure your visit to New Orleans will be lovely," Harlow chimed in.

There was a rustling sound, and Harlow laughed. I guessed she'd snatched the phone from Max.

"Mari knows I'm worried about her," Max said defensively in the background.

"No one likes a lecture, Max," Harlow countered. "Enjoy your time there, Mari."

Max's tone was warmer when his voice returned at full volume. "Okay, apologies for the lecture. I worry about you, and I want you to be safe."

"I know you do, and I appreciate it. I'm sure we'll head back to Nash's office—"

"We're going right now," Nash interjected.

"And I'll take care of the credit freeze right away."

Nash spoke again. "As soon as Brett realizes he can't use any of those shiny new credit cards, he'll figure out that Mari knows what's up."

Chapter Thirteen

NASH

After I got Mari set up in one of the conference rooms at my office, I went into my own office and immediately called Max. While I completely respected Mari, I didn't want to frighten her. My concern about Brett had skyrocketed after learning he put a tracking device on her phone.

Max answered immediately. "I'm guessing there's a reason you wanted to call me without my sister."

"Look, I don't want to freak her out any more than is necessary. You and I both know that there's no surprises with everything concerning the money side of this situation. But Brett showed up at my office building last night. The tracking device is bullshit. How do you think Mari will handle it if I ask her to let my guy Trent take a look at her phone?

The only reason he found the other tracker is through a reverse trace to Brett's old phone. Brett's kind of savvy, but not as savvy as my guy," I said grimly.

"I'm in Alaska right now. Harlow and I just got back from a trip, but I can be on a plane tomorrow if you need me to help with this in person," Max said.

"I think you can help from where you are. I can make sure Mari is safe. If I have to, I'll bring her to my place. I'm guessing she might not appreciate that. I don't think she'd have taken me up on the offer of a place to stay if she hadn't been flat broke."

"In case you haven't noticed, my sister is stubborn as hell. She refuses to take any help from me," Max said dryly.

I laughed. "I've got a sister, so I get it. Look, you stay put in Alaska. We can coordinate from a distance. Let me get you the investigator's number so y'all can chat. I'll ask Mari about her phone this afternoon. She didn't say much about it, but it's clear Brett showing up last night shook her up."

After I recited Trent's number, Max commented, "Do me a favor, and promise you'll call me if anything else weird happens."

"You didn't need to ask, and it's not a favor—I'll call you. In the meantime, I'll make sure Trent knows who you are."

———

"Where are we going?" Mari asked as I hooked a left along on an old country highway.

"I'm taking you to a special spot along the Mississippi River."

"So, you grew up around here?"

"Yes, ma'am."

"Oh, for God's sake, don't call me ma'am."

"Okay, darlin'."

When I stole a glance sideways at Mari, her cheeks flushed slightly, and a throaty laugh escaped.

Fuck me. Mari was too damn sexy. She could recite the alphabet in that raspy voice of hers, and it would turn me on. Hell, she turned me on just by breathing in my presence.

"Let's get specific. Did you grow up right in New Orleans?"

"Not downtown, but on the outskirts. As I mentioned, my daddy was a shrimp fisherman. He worked his tail off, back when you could make decent money off of it. I might have money now, but don't go thinking I grew up with it. We got by, but that was about it. He worked seasonally doing construction in between shrimp season, while my mama was a preschool teacher. She loved those little kids."

"Are they retired?"

"I practically had to beat them into retirement,

but they finally did. My mom still does a little day-care on the side for friends and family because she can't help herself. But my daddy, well, his body is damn near worn out. He's worked hard his whole life. I'm glad to be able to support them. I bought them a nice place, but they would only let me get it so nice. Anyway, tell me about you. I know Max, but all I know about him is he kicks butt at security and makes a ton of money."

Mari laughed softly. "Yeah, Max is the money-maker in our family. Like you, we didn't grow up with much money. Our father has his own business as a mechanic in a garage right beside the house where we grew up. My mom was also a teacher. She finally retired a few years back, but she still does substitute teaching whenever they need it."

"And how'd you get into your job?"

I felt her shrug. "Sort of by accident, although I do like it. I had a crush on a guy in college." When I looked sideways, I saw her roll her eyes. "He was all right, but not worth sticking around. I got paid for doing stories at the university paper. He quit, and I stayed there. I got another job and ended up in grad school. Here I am now. I don't make a ton of money, but it pays the bills, and it's flexible."

"What's your plan? Anything keeping you in San Francisco?"

Mari was quiet for a moment. I slowed as I turned

down a narrow road and stole another look at her. She looked tense, with her shoulders held up and lines bracketing her mouth. "I don't know," she finally said. "Brett screwed me over on my lease. Fucking asshole. Max and Harlow live in San Francisco part-time, but he's in Alaska a lot too. It's not like he needs to be in one place for his business. I've already picked up some jobs, including one here. It's a fluffy piece on local inns, but people love those kinds of stories. I'm going to start with Creek's End Inn. I already talked to Hannah, so I'm planning to go out tomorrow."

"Need a ride?"

"I can handle it. I'm picking up a rental to-morrow morning. My job will cover it. How about you work, and let me know what's next on the agenda for our tour tomorrow afternoon?"

"You got it."

Mari fell quiet as the trees opened up. "Oh wow," she breathed. "This is beautiful."

The narrow road we were on opened up to a field. The Mississippi stretched ahead with cypress trees dotting the shoreline and Spanish moss swaying lazily in the soft breeze. I came to a stop on the edge of the grassy field.

Mari threw her seatbelt off and clambered out quickly. I followed as she walked to stand beside a picnic table situated under the shade of an old live oak.

"Is this a public place?" she asked when she glanced up at me.

"No, darlin'. It's part of the property I bought for my parents."

"Wow, it's incredible here."

Mari spun in a slow circle before walking closer to the shoreline. The scent of gardenias filled the air. Gulls called, and the river drifted slowly in front of us. This portion of the property was on a bluff above the river.

I paused at Mari's side. "I love it here," I commented.

"It's hard not to love it. I imagine it's different for you because this is where you grew up."

Glancing down at her, I nodded. "It feels like home to me. Always will."

When she looked back toward the water, I closed my eyes and took a breath. Since it was mid-afternoon, the day's heat was at its peak. The languid air clung to my skin, but I didn't mind. Under the generous shade of the trees, I let the peace of this place wash over me. Although I hadn't grown up in this specific spot, everything about it felt familiar.

I'd spent many a day when I was a boy near the shores of the Mississippi, playing in the water and getting called back whenever a storm rolled in.

When I opened up my eyes, I felt Mari's gaze. Turning to face her, I took a moment to absorb her. She had her dark hair pulled up into a knot. It had been down earlier, but now she had a pen stuck through it. Several loose tendrils curled against her neck. Lifting a hand, I brushed a lock off her cheek, feeling it slide through my fingers when I tucked it behind her ear. "How am I doing so far at giving you a good week in New Orleans?"

Her eyes darkened to navy as she looked at me. "You're doing very well. Under the circumstances, that's remarkable."

"I'm sorry about everything Brett's doing. We're going to stop it."

Anger tightened my chest. The feeling spun into the ever-present desire that ran like a live wire through my body whenever I was near Mari.

"Not that I need to point this out, but none of this is your fault, Nash. I can't tell you how much I appreciate your help. Between you and Max, I know it'll all be okay. In the meantime, you're making me fall in love with New Orleans."

As we stood there, the air felt electrified—snapping and crackling around us. I couldn't have stopped myself from kissing Mari if I wanted. As she watched me, her tongue darted out, dragging across her bottom lip.

Stepping closer, Mari's scent drifted around me —that hint of vanilla and some kind of flower. It was intoxicating. I slid my hand around to cup her nape. When her breath drew in and caught in her throat, lust sizzled through me.

I waited for a beat—because I didn't want to be alone in this. She bit her lip. "Kiss me, Nash."

I was *all* about taking that kind of order from Mari. Then, she was arching into me and yanking me down, her mouth opening sweetly the moment our lips collided.

Nash's palm slid down my back to rest at the dip of my waist. His tongue stroked against mine, and I gasped into our kiss. Nash was beyond tempting. With his muscled body right there for the taking, I let one hand map his chest while I slid the other up and gripped the corded muscles of his back. I wanted to climb him like he was my personal tree.

Oh my God, the man could kiss. His lips molded to mine as he set out to drive me to madness with nothing more than his mouth. Our kiss was a heated mix of hot, wet, and deep as his tongue teased mine. He pulled back and nipped at my bottom lip. He dusted kisses along my jaw before finding his way back to my mouth again.

He slipped his thigh between my knees, and I became achingly aware of the slick desire at my core. I was out of my mind with need and melting like butter by the time he lifted his head.

Out of nowhere, I heard the sound of voices. "I could've sworn I saw Nash driving down here."

A man's voice carried to us. I jumped away from Nash. "Who's that?" I whispered frantically.

Nash's low chuckle sent goosebumps chasing over my skin. "Sounds like my parents came for a walk. They must've seen me drive past their house. Don't worry."

If I weren't already flustered enough from Nash's dreamy kiss, the unexpected appearance of his parents only added to it. He slid his arm around my waist, his hand coming to rest just above the curve of my hip.

Although my body delighted in his closeness, and I savored his steady presence, I didn't want to create the wrong impression. "Nash!" I whispered frantically.

His hazel eyes angled to mine, and he arched a brow in a silent question.

"It's your parents! They're going to think we're together or something."

There was no further chance to discuss *that* issue because they stepped through the trees. Nash's father was an older, weathered version of him. His hair was the same dark blond, but it was flecked with silver rather than gold. His eyes crinkled at the corners with a warm smile as they approached us. He moved with a similar natural grace, albeit slower and with a slight limp.

Nash's mother, simply put, was lovely. She smiled warmly between us. "Well, hey, Nash," she drawled, her accent soft.

The rounded vowels of her words soothed me, although my heart was pounding along rapidly in my chest. Her hair was white and cut short, curling softly around her ears. Her dark brown eyes were curious as she looked me over from head to toe. She had a slender build and gave off a librarian vibe with her glasses.

"Hey, Mom, Dad," Nash said, entirely at ease. "This is my friend, Mari Channing." He still had his arm around my waist, and I felt a subtle squeeze from where his palm rested there. "Mari, this is my mother, Sandra, and my father, Nash. You can just call him Senior."

Nash's father chuckled. "He likes everyone to call me Senior because we always called him Junior and still do."

Uncertain whether to actually call him Senior or not, I simply smiled. "Nice to meet you both."

"Oh, sweetie," Sandra said, reaching out to place her hand on my shoulder and giving it a gentle squeeze. "He's teasing. We do call him Junior, but only sometimes. It *is* easier if you call his father, Senior. Otherwise, Lord knows people get confused."

"Okay," I murmured.

"What are y'all doing here today?" Sandra asked next.

"Mari's visiting from out of town, and I promised her I'd show her the best of New Orleans. Can't beat this view," Nash replied.

"How nice," Sandra said while Nash's father winked.

"Now, where are you from, Mari?" Sandra asked nicely.

The inquisition wasn't over yet.

"Most recently, San Francisco, but I'm in-between places right now. My trip took an unexpected turn. I'm doing a story on inns around New Orleans," I explained.

Sandra opened her mouth for what I presumed was her next question, but Senior cut in quickly, reaching for her hand. "I'm sure Sandra would love to ask you a million questions, but we need to be going."

Sandra opened her mouth to say something, and he interrupted again before she could even speak. "Remember? I need to get your car in for an oil change. Scheduled that appointment yesterday morning."

Sandra looked from her husband to me, and then Nash. She smiled sweetly. "Oh, that's right. Well, Mari, it was lovely to meet you. Nash, you bring her over for dinner now, okay?"

"We'll see if we have time," he replied, appearing unruffled by this exchange.

Moments later, we watched as they disappeared back into the trees along a path I hadn't noticed when we first walked out here.

After their voices faded, Nash glanced at me with an apologetic smile on his face. "Sorry about that. I didn't expect them to show up."

"They're going to think we're a couple," I muttered.

"Would that be so bad?" he murmured. He kept his hand on my hip as he angled to face me.

My pulse leapt, and I felt a bead of sweat roll down between my breasts. "I mean, not necessarily. But—"

My words were cut off abruptly when Nash leaned down and brushed his lips across mine. He lingered for a moment before nipping lightly on my bottom lip and straightening. "It's hot. Let's go."

Oh, it was hot all right, but it wasn't just the Louisiana heat. Nash had personally incinerated my defenses and lit hundreds of tiny fires inside me.

It was easier to go along than to try to make sense of any of this. As he turned, his hand slid off my waist to catch mine.

I asked, "What now?"

"I thought I would take you for a drive so you can see the countryside, and then take you to dinner in the French Quarter."

Chapter Fifteen

NASH

Mari sat beside me, laughing at something Johnny said. The jazz band served as our background music. The noises from the crowd filling the small restaurant and bar hummed around us.

All the while, I was just trying to get a grip. Today had been a unique form of torture for me. Playing tour guide for Mari was testing my willpower and discipline.

When I told her I wanted to bring her down for dinner at Johnny's Bar, she'd insisted she needed to change first. It didn't seem to matter what Mari wore as far as my body was concerned. Yet, she'd taken things up a notch tonight.

An unsuspecting fool, I'd stopped in at the office to check in with Lydia while Mari went upstairs to change. When Mari came back downstairs, I choked on a swallow of coffee, which got me a sly grin from Lydia. She wore a flirty skirt that twirled at her knees and a silky blouse with low-heeled sandals.

Johnny was drawn away to help another customer, and Mari spun on her stool to face me. She was still smiling, and her cheeks were flushed. "I'm so glad I stayed," she announced.

"Yeah?"

"Yes, and thanks to you, I'm getting the best of New Orleans. Brunch this morning was divine. Even though I'm still a little mortified about your parents, that spot by the river was beautiful and made it worth the embarrassment. Everywhere else you took me today was spectacular, and now we're here for dinner." She pressed a hand to her chest. "If you didn't notice, I do love good food."

"I might've noticed that," I murmured. "Glad to be of service."

Mari's blouse wasn't fitted, but the slip and slide of the silk when she moved to lift her margarita gave me a tease of her cleavage. I'd been hard for most of the night since we'd arrived. The place was crowded, so we'd eaten right here at the bar, sharing oysters.

My eyes tracked her motion when she tilted her chin back. I wanted to lean forward and drag my tongue along the side of her neck. Tearing my gaze away, my eyes landed on the silky skin of her thigh. Fuck me. There was nowhere safe to look. Her skirt had ridden up to rest halfway up her thighs where she sat on the stool.

Before I thought about it, I was reaching to tug her stool a little closer to mine. She lowered her drink, setting the glass on the bar. When her eyes met mine, her pupils were dilated—the blue was dark in the dim lighting of the bar.

It was crowded here, yet we were tucked in the corner, right against the wall. I watched her with my heart drumming hard and fast, and my cock swelling. I wanted her. Hell, I was near to desperation from the fierce need.

In a hot second, Mari's plush lips were inches from mine, and her tongue swiped out to dab in one corner. Not thinking had me dipping my head and brushing my lips across hers before dusting kisses down her neck. The sound of her breath catching in her throat and a soft little gasp escaping was like a sharp spur driving in the flanks of my desire.

"Nash!" she gasped again when I nipped lightly at her ear lobe.

"Hmm?" I murmured against her skin as I slid a palm up her silky thigh.

"There are people everywhere," she whispered when I lifted my head to look into her eyes.

"We're just kissing."

When I teased my fingers over the silk between her thighs, she bit her lip and shook her head slightly. "It's not just kissing."

"Tell me to stop, and I promise I will."

I didn't wait for her reply and slid my hand away, fully taking it off her warm, tempting skin.

Mari bit her lip again, driving those spurs deeper as the need in me strained to be let loose.

"I don't want you to stop," she rasped after a long, heavy moment.

Leaning forward, I brushed my lips across hers again and let my palms slide over her skin. I almost let out a growl at her moan when I trailed my fingers over the silk between her thighs, gratified to find it wet. As deep as my desire ran for Mari, I didn't want to be alone in it.

Everything around us receded as I hooked a finger over the edge of her panties. I watched her when I dragged my fingers through her slick folds. Her channel rippled around me as I drove two fingers into her slick, clenching heat.

"Nash..."

"What?" My voice was tight, like the rest of my body, as I tried to hold myself back.

"I thought you were a gentleman," she choked out as I slipped my fingers back before driving deep inside her again.

"Only sometimes."

This was crazy and decidedly public, so I wasn't going to drag it out. With one of my arms curled around her waist and the other shielded by her flirty skirt, I knew no one could see what I was doing, but still.

I swirled my thumb around her swollen clit, and she gasped. Her channel clamped tight around my fingers. She choked out my name as her eyes fell closed, and her orgasm rippled through her entire body.

Chapter Sixteen

MARI

Opening my eyes, I sat there as my body rippled with the aftershocks of my climax. I was literally stunned with pleasure as Nash withdrew his touch from the very core of me and put my panties back in place. The sounds around us gradually filtered into my awareness.

Nash's eyes ensnared mine, and prickly awareness chased over my skin. I didn't know what to think of what was happening—with me even letting this happen. It felt as if we'd known each other for far longer than we had in terms of time.

Nash leaned forward, pressing an almost chaste kiss on my temple. "How late do you want to stay?"

My heartbeat echoed through my body. All I knew was I wanted more, so much more that it made me feel a little crazy. I finally looked away from him, taking in the people around the bar. The jazz music rolled along with a sensuous beat, and the hum of strangers' voices punctured the haze of lust clouding my thoughts.

Looking back to Nash, I replied, "Let's go. Now."

His eyes searched mine, and it felt as if he were trying to suss out what I was thinking. I wished him luck on that because clarity was millions of miles away for me.

Only moments later, his hand was resting at the base of my spine as he guided me through the people crowding the streets of downtown New Orleans. Glancing up, I asked, "Is it ever not busy here?"

"For the most part, no. The weather is usually warm, so it's a good place to visit all year round."

As we turned down the cross street that intersected the road where Nash's offices were, and by extension where I was staying, a sense of uneasiness crept through me. As I looked around, I saw a vehicle parked on the opposite corner. I looked up at Nash to find his eyes narrowed on the same car, his gaze quiet and assessing.

"It's just a car," I thought to myself.

"So it is." It was only when Nash replied that I realized I'd spoken aloud.

Glancing up at him again, I asked, "I think I'm being weird, but that car freaks me out."

"You're not being weird. Trust your gut. It's not the car that has my nerves on edge. It's the guy standing on the opposite street corner. Don't look." I quickly averted my gaze as I'd almost reflexively looked in that direction as soon as he spoke.

"What is it about the guy?" I kept my voice close to a whisper.

"I'm guessing he's from one of the gangs here in New Orleans."

My breath hissed through my teeth in a startled inhalation. "How would you even know that?"

"Let's talk once we get inside."

We walked in silence as we turned onto the next block. My heart was drumming out a fast, nervous beat, and my stomach churned. I didn't manage to take a full breath until Nash punched in the security code on my door after we were already in the building and upstairs.

I walked quickly across the room, my arms wrapping tight around my waist as I stared out into the darkness. Spinning back, I found Nash standing a few feet away, his gaze pensive as he watched me.

"You okay?"

"I don't know." Realizing I would be visible to anyone outside in the darkness, I tapped the button that closed the automatic shades on the windows. The very windows I had loved this morning with the bright sunlight splashing into the room felt menacing now. I felt like a fish in a bowl.

"I only told you my concern about that man be-cause I promised myself I wasn't going to hide things from you."

"Mind answering my question now?"

"Mari, I was born and raised here. I never ran with any gang, but I didn't grow up rich, or in the best neighborhood. It was pretty rough and tumble. I know what's what and who's who. Since I work in real estate, I also keep my ear to the ground about everything, and that includes deals in the less desir-able parts of town. Gangs have money, and they buy property. I'm pretty sure that was a bodyguard for one of the higher-ups in a local gang. His illegal ac-tivities bump into perfectly legal activities, including real estate investments."

"So maybe they're just scouting out the neigh-borhood for some property?" I asked, hopefully.

Nash shook his head slowly. "Definitely not. I own everything on these two blocks. I bought it up five years ago."

Dread coated my insides. Nash's next question did nothing to help matters.

"You don't happen to know if Brett was having some financial troubles? Something where he might have needed a loan in a pinch?"

"Well, he clearly needed money because he was fucking me over by taking credit cards out. I'm not sure I understand what you're asking."

"I don't mean running up bills or getting out new

credit cards for start-up funding, which was his superficial reason for wanting to meet with me. Did he owe somebody money that involved a deadline?"

"I don't know. I really don't. I'm beginning to realize there was a lot I didn't know about Brett. Why are you asking that specifically?"

"Because the guy I'm talking about—not the bodyguard, but the guy he works for—is known for short term loans. A loan shark, if you will. If Brett owes them money, that would explain a lot of the stuff he's been pulling since you two got here. I'm not asking to be nosy, but how serious were you with him?"

I let out a shaky sigh as I paced back and forth in front of the shaded windows. "For the last few months, we hardly saw each other, and I honestly thought we were just dying on the vine. Like I inconveniently mentioned before, it's been months since we were, well, intimate. When Brett asked me about this trip, I thought maybe..." I closed my eyes and shook my head as I came to a stop. Opening my eyes, I continued, "I don't know. I guess I thought maybe this trip could be the opportunity we needed to reset our relationship. Lord knows why I would even want that. It's not like things were great with us. I can be stubborn, and I haven't had the best luck with men, so I guess the bar was low."

"Brett was a fucking idiot," Nash said flatly. "That's not why I was asking. I'm just trying to figure out if you might've had some clue what the hell he was doing." Pausing, he slipped his phone out of his pocket. "I need to make a quick call."

I watched as he tapped a number on the screen before lifting the phone to his ear. Restless, I crossed the room into the kitchen area and poured myself a glass of water. I was starting to get scared. Correction: I *was* scared.

Nash's questions made too much sense. I might not have known why Brett needed a loan, but it certainly explained a lot of his actions—his out of the blue suggestion for this trip, cutting off all contact, running my credit cards up, and then trying to find me again.

"Hey Trent, it's Nash. I'm with Mari Channing right now. I just walked her back to the apartment where she's staying in the residential floor of my office building. I think one of the guys from the payday lender guy, Fast Money Now, is out on the street. I don't have anything other than a gut feeling, but it would explain a lot about why Brett was running up her credit cards and trying to get access to more."

Nash paused while whoever was on the other end of the line said something. "Just look into it for me, would you? I realize there will be no record, but I know you have some contacts."

There was another silence, and then Nash's reply sent dread spinning in tight, cold circles around my heart. "I know. I got extra security lined up after Brett showed up here, but this is no fucking joke if he's in it with these guys and owes them money." Another pause and then, "Thanks, man. Call me any time, day or night, once you find out anything."

Nash ended the call and looked at me. "I need to loop your brother in."

I nodded while panic cascaded through me in icy waterfalls.

I listened as he again explained the situation to Max before glancing at me. "I think she's okay. Pulling the phone away from his ear, he asked, "Do you want to talk to Max?"

Knowing my brother would start blowing up my phone if I didn't talk to him, I held my hand out. As soon as Nash passed his phone over, I lifted it to my ear. "Hey, Max."

"It's going to be fine, Mari. Stick with Nash. We've already agreed we'll pay off whatever Brett owes if that's what's going on."

"Oh my God, don't do that!" I sputtered.

"Mari, if they think they can get to Brett through you, you are not safe. Trust me, I don't want to pay anything off for Brett, but your safety is worth it to me. It will also send a message to them you're off-limits. As soon as we know you're safe, we'll figure out what to do after that."

Uncertain what else to say, I mumbled, "Thanks, Max."

After I handed the phone back to Nash, I got more water while he talked to Max some more.

My chest felt tight, and unease rippled through me in little tremors. I couldn't believe Brett might have put me in this situation. It had been enough to try to absorb what an asshole he was, but to realize he might've put me in genuine danger was shocking. I didn't like the feeling, not one bit.

I heard Nash saying goodbye to Max and felt him walk up beside me where I stood in front of the windows. With the shades closed, there was nothing for me to look at, so I was studying a photograph mounted on the wall beside the windows. It was of a shrimp boat silhouetted against a watercolor sunset of tangerine and pink with the Gulf waters shimmering a reflection of colors.

Nash stopped beside me and was quiet for a few moments. As unsettled as I was, the quiet helped. It soothed the anxiety tinged with panic inside my chest. His palm landed between my shoulder blades, and I could feel the heat of it through the thin silk of my blouse.

"Don't worry, Max and I have a plan."

Restless, almost driven to move by the jumble of feelings bouncing around inside of me, I turned to face him. "Don't worry?" I took a shaky breath before I could continue. "You're telling me Brett might be tangled up with some kind of loan shark. What kind of plan could you even have?"

Nash regarded me quietly. I didn't like having him see me like this. I already felt like an idiot over Brett. The recognition that I could be in genuine danger made me sick and I felt like an even bigger fool.

Tearing my eyes from his, I began pacing again. Nash stayed where he was, yet he turned to face me. "Mari, I know these guys. I'm not friends with them, but I'm a businessman in New Orleans, and I grew up here. I know just about everyone."

Stopping my pacing, I threw my hands up, letting them fall abruptly. "What are you gonna do?"

"If necessary, we'll pay them off. They just want their money. In the meantime, Max and I are going to track down Brett and work with the police to file charges. That's what needs to happen."

I took a deep breath, pressing the heels of my hands into my eyes as I tried to calm down. When I opened my eyes, Nash was standing by the counter, pouring a glass of whiskey.

"Come here," he said.

"I don't think alcohol is going to make me feel better," I muttered as I slowly approached the counter.

He slid his hips onto a stool and tugged the other one out slightly before patting it with his hand. "Just take a few sips."

He poured another glass of whiskey as I sat on the stool beside him. Lifting the tumbler, I took a swallow. "Oh, this is good," I murmured as the liquor slid in a rich and smooth burn across my tongue.

"New Orleans has plenty of distilleries. We do whiskey right."

It did take the jagged edge off of my nerves as I took a few more swallows. Looking over at him, I commented, "Bet you didn't realize just how much of an asshole I dated."

"I'll tell you something my grandma told me when I was a little boy. I never forgot it," he began.

"Are these words of wisdom?" I teased.

"I suppose, but it's not my wisdom. Back when I first started up my business, I was young, and hungry for chances. Along the way, I made a few mistakes in my partnerships. I also dated a woman who totally screwed me over in a business deal. After that happened, I felt like I wasn't cut out to chase after more than I had before. Gram told me the way people treat each other is a reflection of them, not you. Even though I got screwed over more than once, it didn't say anything about me. It said something about the person and what they did. Don't get me wrong; there are always lessons to be learned. But what Brett did is no reflection on you. You were a decent person, and you trusted him. Nothing wrong with that. I get it, maybe you feel like an idiot. But Brett's the asshole here. You're not the idiot."

I took another swallow of my whiskey, and my

nerves settled a bit more. Maybe it was numbness, but I wasn't drunk. I just needed something to dull my jangly nerves.

"It's always easier to see that for somebody else, isn't it?" I commented.

"Always."

"What did Max say?" I asked.

"He doesn't think you're an idiot. He thinks you wish for the best in everyone."

I hadn't realized just how tense my shoulders were until I felt them relax slightly. Nash's words helped unwind the tension bundled there. I took another swallow of my whiskey before I set the glass down. "Your grandma seems like a smart woman."

"She was, but that wasn't my point. Everyone feels foolish sometimes."

I idly traced my fingertip along the square tiles on the counter. "How worried do I need to be about these loan shark guys you're talking about?"

When I risked a glance in Nash's direction, his gaze was shuttered. That told me all I needed to know. He was trying too hard not to appear concerned. He was worried.

Spinning on my stool to face him directly, I added, "Be straight with me. Anything else, and I'll assume the worst."

Nash took a swallow of his drink. "These are men who get what they want, and they don't exactly color inside the lines in the process."

"The lines being the law?"

Nash nodded somberly. "Exactly." There was a heavy pause, and then, "Max doesn't want me to let you stay alone."

"Are you serious?"

He nodded again. "I understand his concern. You can stay here, or come to my place. I was thinking tonight I would sleep on the couch here because we already have security set up. I can get everything lined up for my house by tomorrow. I have a security system, but I rarely have people on the property."

A chill gusted through me. It felt as if an icy breeze passed through the inside of my body. This was getting too *real*.

"Jesus. Are you serious?" I repeated.

"Look, as soon as they know you're connected to me, it will probably help. Maybe they've already figured it out from seeing me with you tonight. They won't harm you, but they might use you for leverage to get to Brett." As my brain was grappling with that insanity, Nash continued, "What do you say? I'll crash on the couch here tonight. I'll make arrangements for you to move out to my place tomorrow."

I bit my lip, caught between two impulses. I didn't like being told where I should stay, or what I should do. Yet, I was scared, and I knew it was probably the smart choice to stay with Nash. There was also a third impulse—the one that couldn't forget the intensely sexy and hot as hell moment in the bar with Nash. I wanted to forget all of this. I knew I could forget it in the heat of raw desire.

"Mari?" Nash prompted.

Lifting my eyes, I searched his and saw the rapid beat of his pulse along the strong column of his neck. "Okay."

"Okay, what?"

"You stay here tonight. Then, I guess either you keep staying here, or we go to your place. Which option is safer?"

"My place."

"How come?"

"Because I'm the only person who lives there. We have security on site here, and the building is monitored, but other people live here. The residential section has thirty condos. Security fields any number of people coming in to see other people living here. No matter how you slice it, there are more contingencies to manage here."

"Okay. We'll go to your place tomorrow."

Nash stared at me, almost as if he wasn't sure I meant it.

"Are you surprised I gave in that easily?" I was trying to tease, anything to distract me from my jittery state.

After a beat, he lifted his shoulder in a light shrug. "I suppose I am."

As we sat there in the quiet, it felt as if the air began to warm with little sparks bouncing between us. I needed Nash. My confusing, not-so-smart lust for him, could serve more than one purpose. I could slake my need and lose myself in his strength and the security I felt in his arms.

We weren't sitting very far apart, and I leaned forward, trailing my fingertip along the edge of his jaw. The feel of his slight stubble prickling on my skin was a tiny sensation bouncing into others, like atoms colliding, each explosion multiplying from the last.

"What are you doing, Mari?" Nash nearly growled.

"You're the one who got me all hot and bothered back at the bar. Now you're here, and apparently, you're spending the night."

I couldn't believe how bold I was with him, yet everything seemed to come easy with Nash. Although my nerves were on fire, he was my touchstone in the midst of the tumult stirring me up inside.

Chapter Seventeen

NASH

Looking into Mari's eyes, I knew my desire for her was reflected in mine. Electric need pulsed through my body, and my hands literally itched to reach for her.

Yet, I was wrestling with a belated sense of honor. Yes, I'd been the one who couldn't resist touching her and tasting her in the bar. But now, I knew she was riled up inside. A mingled sense of fear and restlessness was palpable as it emanated from her.

Of course, I also just got off the phone with her older brother. While we might not be best friends, I definitely considered him a friend and trusted business partner. Although Max had asked me directly to stay with Mari so she wasn't alone, I sincerely doubted he meant for me to fuck his little sister.

I managed a breath and caught her hand in mine. "Maybe that was a mistake." Touching Mari was not exactly helpful for the state of my body. I managed a slow breath and shackled my need. "Not now."

Mari's eyes narrowed. "Not now, what?"

I closed my eyes for a moment, doing my damnedest to get my shit together inside. Opening them, I saw anger flashing in hers. It didn't help me to contemplate how passionate she was by nature.

"I know I started something earlier, but I don't think tonight is the night to let things go further. You're scared, and—I can't believe I'm saying this— I promised your brother I'd make sure you stayed safe. I seriously don't think he would appreciate me taking advantage of that situation."

Mari yanked her hand free from mine and pushed her stool back abruptly as she stood, once again pacing the room. "Great, now you're bringing my brother into this? This isn't about you taking advantage of me. Plus, you're the one who took things that direction earlier. Your sense of honor is a little late."

She had a point. I rolled my head from side to side, trying to lessen the tension gathering. Meeting her eyes, I told the plain truth. "Yes, I took things to another level earlier, and I won't lie. I want more, *much* more with you. I don't want this to go further just because you're feeling unsettled and reckless. I know your brother is not your keeper. That said, I just got off the phone with him moments ago, so forgive me for having a conscience."

Mari stopped her pacing, turning and lasering me with her eyes. "What do you mean you want more?"

"I don't know exactly. But I know I don't want this to be a one and done kind of thing with you. I don't think you'll argue the point with me that there's definitely chemistry between us."

Mari was quiet, and I could hear her soft exhalation when she shook her head. I didn't know what passed through her mind, but she finally shrugged. "Fine, I'm going to bed. Do you need a blanket on the couch?"

"No," I said slowly, a shaft of regret piercing me. Although I was trying to be a gentleman, I didn't like the idea of her being on the other side of the door in a bed with me out here alone.

———

I couldn't say it was easy, but I managed to fall into a restless sleep on the couch. When a noise woke me, I rolled up instantly, my eyes scanning the shadowy apartment. The security keypad still showed the door was locked, and there was nothing amiss.

It was only when my phone vibrated again that I realized security was attempting to contact me. Lifting it, I tapped my phone screen quickly. "What's up?"

"Mr. Reynolds, you asked us to notify you if there were any concerns tonight. We had someone attempt to gain entry to the building. They reported they were visiting the tenant across the hall from Miss Channing. We're aware the tenant is out of town."

"Now?" I asked. A glance at my phone screen let me know it was two a.m.

"Yes, sir. Obviously, we turned them away. To clarify, they didn't even come in the entryway. They tried to buzz in from the outside."

I was instantly alert, my body vibrating with tension. I didn't want to be right with my potential suspicions about Brett getting tangled up with a loan shark. I kept those concerns to myself. "Thank you for the notice. Please contact me immediately if anything else comes up."

Just as I was setting my phone back on the coffee table beside the couch, the door to Mari's bedroom swung open. The lamp in the corner was on, casting her in shadow from behind.

"Is everything okay?" she asked, her voice raspy from sleep.

I silently cursed that she'd heard me take the call. "Everything's fine."

"Who's calling you at this hour?"

"Mari—"

She stepped out of the bedroom. Unfortunately

for me, I could see the swell of her breasts pressing against the cotton of her T-shirt.

"I doubt anyone would call you about business at this hour. What is it? Trying to hide things from me doesn't help me stay calm," she pressed.

I needed a serious distraction to keep me from standing from the couch, walking to her, and carting her into the bedroom. I thought perhaps being honest with her would do the trick.

"That was the lead security guy on duty tonight. I asked them to call if anything unusual blipped on the radar."

Mari took another step into the living room, and I silently bit back a curse. The light angling through the doorway of her bedroom cast her body in silhouette through her T-shirt. It fell only halfway down her thighs, and it was all I could do not to wonder what she wore underneath. I didn't need my eyes to linger on the lush curves of her hips and the way her waist dipped in only to lift higher to her breasts. My cock was rock hard in a second.

Mari had insisted on getting me a blanket and pillow, so I'd shucked off my slacks and was only wearing my boxers and a T-shirt. I tucked the blanket over my waist.

"What were they calling about?" she prompted.

"Someone attempted to pay a visit to the apartment across the hallway from this one. They even gave the name of the tenant there. However, the tenant happens to be out of town."

I heard the soft gasp escape from Mari's lips and instantly regretted being that direct.

She closed the distance between us just as I started to stand. She sat down beside me, her hands clasped together over her knees. "Do they know who it was?"

My protective instincts kicked into high gear. I slid an arm around her shoulders, hating how stiffly she held herself. "They didn't give their names, but our cameras will have everything. I'm sure my security team is already running it through the database to identify who they were. Your brother set up this whole system, or rather his company did. There's no way they're going to get in this building. They're not going to break down your door, Mari. They may not know I'm personally in here with you, but I'm sure they know the building is being monitored."

"Then, what were they doing?"

"These guys operate strategically. My guess is they were just trying to get a lay of the building. For all we know, Brett told them he's staying with you."

Although my brain, or rather my body, shouldn't be reacting under the circumstances, having Mari close to me was sending little lightning strikes of lust through my body. I moved my hand up and down her back in slow passes, hoping to soothe her.

She let out another sigh. "I can't believe this."

When she turned to look at me, everything froze for a moment. My breath caught, and my heartbeat stuttered before lunging. I tried to remind myself I wanted to slow this down, somehow do this the right way. But I could barely hear my own thoughts over the rush of need pounding through me.

Mari, in nothing more than a thin T-shirt with her scent spinning around me like gossamer threads and catching me in its web, was too much for my rational, honorable mind. All I knew was I wanted her.

Her tongue darted out, sliding across her bottom lip. I thought she whispered my name, but I couldn't be certain. The sound of her breath catching in her throat as she leaned toward me, pierced my hazy mind and electricity sizzled down my spine.

In a fiery second, she cupped my cheek and drew me to her mouth. Although I could've tried to convince myself she started it, that was an irrelevant detail. Because just as she arched up, I leaned down.

When our lips met, my body took that hit like a jolt straight into my veins. Mari was a drug for me. She was mine and mine alone, and I was already addicted.

Her lips were soft and warm when she teased her tongue against mine. I scrambled to grasp the reins of my control. I pulled back, just a whisper away from her.

"Are you sure this is what you want, Mari?" I asked in a gruff whisper.

It felt as if everything in me was leaning forward, just about to fall over the edge of a waterfall. The force of the current pushing me was almost impossible to withstand. I waited for her answer as her lashes swept up, and she caught my gaze.

"Absolutely."

That single whispered word in Mari's sexy, raspy voice, tipped me over the edge.

And then, we dove into our kiss together, a tangle of lips, teeth, and tongue. In a matter of seconds, I pulled Mari into my lap. She was a warm, silky soft bundle of curves, and I couldn't get enough of her.

Tearing my mouth free from hers, I pressed wet, open kisses along her jaw, and caught her earlobe in my teeth. Satisfaction washed through me when she shivered, and her skin rose in goosebumps in the wake of my touch.

Mari's hands gripped my shoulders, sliding down over my biceps before one palm hooked on the hem of my T-shirt and skimmed against my skin under the fabric. I never even thought much about the subtle feel of a woman's touch. Her touch was like the sparks from flint striking against stone, every spark falling into the fire already threatening to engulf us both.

Meanwhile, I slid my palms up her sides, savoring her ragged gasp and the murmur of my name. I already knew what she felt like at her core, but I needed to touch her desperately. Pressing her thighs apart, I expected to encounter her silky panties.

I knew she wore silk. I lost my damn mind at the bar earlier tonight when I felt that wet silk between her legs. Perhaps I'd simply tricked myself into thinking I saw the silhouette of her panties when she stood in the doorway only moments ago. I was startled to find nothing but her bare, wet pussy.

"Fuck, Mari," I murmured against her skin as I was tracing her collarbone with my tongue.

"What?" she asked on a gasp when her hips arched into my fingers.

"You're so fucking wet."

I drew my fingers out and lifted them. I needed to taste her essence.

Her eyes were on me, her lips parted when I sucked my fingers, savoring the sweet elixir of her desire. I roughly yanked her shirt up and over her head. I *needed* to feel her against me.

"You have too many clothes on," Mari murmured, her tone bossy.

"We can remedy that right quick."

Shifting, I hooked my hand on the back of my T-shirt behind my neck and tossed it aside. Mari shimmied back onto my lap, yanking my boxers down just enough for my cock to spring free. Her palm curled around it, lightly gripping at the base before sliding up. Her eyes locked to mine as she swiped the drop of pre-cum rolling out the tip with her thumb before she licked it clean.

It was a fucking miracle I could think at all. Through the haze of raw need driving me, I reached for my jeans, where I'd draped them over the edge of the sofa. I yanked out my wallet and a condom so fast that everything else in it fell across the floor.

"Hurry," Mari demanded as she rocked her hips, her slick folds sliding over the underside of my cock.

I rolled the condom on ruthlessly fast. In another second, I was gripping Mari's hips when she rose up. Reaching between us to position my cock at her entrance, my fingers pressed into the soft give of her flesh as I held her still. "I want to feel every inch," I murmured.

In return, Mari let out a low cry as I slowly breached her entrance. It took every ounce of discipline I had not to slam into her, but I wanted it slow.

Her core sheathed my cock slowly in a tight, silky clench. She finally settled down over me, wiggling her hips slightly and almost pushing me over the edge, an edge which I was barely clinging to with my fingertips.

She let out a satisfied little hum. "Oh, Nash," she murmured. "I needed this. I needed you."

My heart tumbled in my chest. I didn't quite know what to do with the sense of raw, pure satisfaction that gripped me at hearing her say aloud that she needed me.

I needed this. I needed you.

In the shadowed light, I stared into Nash's eyes, my words reverberating in my mind. We were joined as intimately as two people could be with my core stretched to its max and my heartbeat racing. I could barely catch my breath and felt as if I'd been tossed into the air and was free-falling.

I was awash in sensation, and I didn't know how to get my bearings, the feelings were so intense. The only thing I could hold onto, the only touchstone in this swirling storm of sensation, piercing pleasure and need, was Nash.

I could feel the calloused surface of his palms, where they pressed against my hips. His hold both secure and steadfast. "You've got me. All of me," he rasped.

My nipples, so tight they ached, grazed over the muscled planes of his chest. The dusting of his hair was yet another sensation spinning into the rest of them. The feel of him filling me was incredible; the stretch decadent and intense.

In tune with each other, we held still for a beat as I adjusted to the feel of him inside me. Nash leaned forward and pressed a hot, open kiss against my neck. Then, we began rocking into each other, a slow, sensual fuck in the darkness. It should've just been sex, but it felt like so much more.

My orgasm was racing upon me quickly from the friction of my swollen clit as it rubbed against the base of Nash's cock. Each deep nudge of his shaft inside of me pushed me closer and closer. The slow pull and glide was intoxicating, the friction sending pleasure spiraling in sharp streaks through me.

"Mari."

The sound of my name in Nash's gravelly drawl brought my eyes open. I watched him as he arched back once and filled me yet again. My orgasm shattered me. I felt as if I were flying to pieces as he held me tight. My entire body shuddered from intense waves of pleasure.

Nash cried my name again in a rough growl. His body went taut as a bow and he trembled against me. His arms wrapped around my back as I fell against his chest and frantically gasped for air.

Pleasure pinged through me and slowed to little

eddies. I gradually became aware of the feel of his hands sliding through the ends of my hair.

In the aftermath, Nash carried me into bed. As I lay languid in his arms, I wondered about how easy this felt. Part of me wanted to tell myself this was nothing more than a rebound, something to soothe my stinging pride. I tumbled into sleep, wrapped in his warm, strong embrace.

Yet, it felt so *easy*, so right. My tendency to worry things to pieces was subdued, if only because I simply couldn't even bring myself to go there. The last thought flickering through my mind before I fell into a deep, comforting sleep was that I couldn't recall ever feeling this good with someone. As restless and as unsettled as I'd been for weeks now, I slept better that night than I had in months.

————

The following morning, I had a relaxing breakfast and coffee interlude with Nash. In spite of the stressors I was facing—my financial situation, and the news that Brett appeared to have stupidly made arrangements with a loan shark that put me in direct danger—I actually felt good.

Once again, the connection I felt with Nash was just so natural and felt so *right*. I didn't quite know what to make of it, so I decided not to worry about it. I certainly had a long list of other worries.

Nash had gone down to his office and returned with a laptop. He was presently working while sipping his coffee. I was busy compiling a list of inns I intended to visit. Using Hannah 's list of recommendations as a starting point, I expanded from there.

My phone chimed on the table where Nash was sitting across from me. Spinning my phone around to glance at the screen, an unfamiliar number blinked at me as it continued to ring.

"Who is it?" Nash asked, his gaze alert.

"I don't recognize the number. Could just be a robocall. Like everyone in the world, I get plenty of those," I said dryly.

Nash sipped his coffee and commented, "Let's see if they leave a message."

Another moment passed after the ringing stopped, and then my phone chimed with a voicemail. I put it on speaker as soon as I realized it was Brett.

Mari, it's Brett. I need you to call me a soon as you get this. Use this number.

My eyes met Nash's across the table. "Well, should I call him back?"

"Absolutely. If you don't mind, I'd like to call him back."

"Feel free. I've about had enough of talking to him."

"Mind if I call from your phone?"

"Of course not."

Nash immediately reached for my phone and tapped to return the call. He put it on speaker, so I could hear the whole thing.

After two rings, Brett answered, "Thanks for calling back so quickly. Look, Mari—"

Nash cut in immediately. "This isn't Mari, it's Nash Reynolds. What do you need?"

"Why the hell are you listening to Mari's messages and calling me back?" Brett asked quickly. I could hear the frustration in his tone and had to bite the insides of my cheeks to keep from snapping at him. As if he had any claim on me, or any right to have an opinion about Nash hearing my messages.

"The better question would be why the hell did you put her at risk?" Nash countered swiftly.

"What the fuck are you talking about? Look, Mari and I are in a relationship. I don't know why you're involved in the situation, but it's none of your damn business."

Catching Nash's eye, I arched a brow in question, and he circled his hand in the air with a *proceed* motion.

I interjected. "Seriously, Brett? It's none of *your* business why Nash is involved. He's helping me because you fucking left me in one hell of a situation. You ran up all my credit cards and opened new ones. In my name. You also fucked me over on the lease on my apartment."

"Mari, you don't understand. I need you to remove that credit freeze, so I can have access to those credit cards. They're jointly in our name."

He was blatantly lying, and I knew it. "Stop lying, Brett. They're solely in my name because we've been doing a little digging, pulling my credit report and I saw them. And no, I'm not lifting the credit freeze. As for acting like we have something here—that there's still a relationship between us—that's total bullshit. We dated for less than a year. In the last few months, for all intents and purposes we were hardly dating, and you damn well know it. I don't know exactly why you're trying to claim differently but it's perfectly clear to me that you were just using me. Now, I'm worried about some loan shark coming after me since you put me smack in the middle of your mess."

Thanks to Nash and what passed between us last night, I'd somehow managed to put my fear around that situation far in the recesses of my thoughts. Saying it aloud brought it back forcefully. Fear shafted through me, and cold dread coated the insides of my stomach.

Without a word, Nash reached over and curled his hand over mine. My hands had gone icy cold, but the warmth of his touch helped me catch my breath and put the brakes on the fear revving inside of me.

Chapter Nineteen

NASH

Mari's hand was icy cold, and I was fucking furious. Not at her, but at Brett and the mess he'd made.

"Brett, Nash here. What the hell is going on?"

Brett sputtered. "I don't know what you're talking about. I just need some money. I had a good investment opportunity, and you passed on it. So now, I'm finding a way to deal with it myself. We don't need you in the middle of this."

"There is no 'we,'" Mari exclaimed. "As soon as we straighten out this mess, I have no intention of talking to you *ever* again."

I squeezed her hand, and she closed her eyes and took a slow breath.

"Brett, here's the deal. Mari's brother is looking into things on the backend. We know you hacked into her bank accounts and falsified applications for credit cards. Last night, I saw a guy who works for a local gang. Specifically, one run by a guy who's well known as a loan shark. He is *not* the kinda guy you screw over. Tell me now if you borrowed money from him, because *if so,* and *if* you can't pay it back on time, you're facing a shit load of trouble. You've put a target on Mari in the process."

Brett's swallow was audible through the phone line. "I didn't realize what kind of business it was. I don't know what the fuck to do," he finally said after a long pause.

"You're a fucking idiot. If you didn't know it before, you can rest assured if no place reputable will issue you a loan, only crooks will. I appreciate your honesty." Mari's eyes had gone wide, but I shook my head. She could talk, but I didn't think it would be helpful at this point. She rolled her eyes and glared daggers at the phone. I continued, "I can be more helpful if I know exactly what the situation is."

After a little bit of bluster, Brett broke it down. He was looking for money for his stupid investment plan and had made promises to a few other investors. As a result, he borrowed money from this guy to the tune of half a million. No shocker, but now it was coming due, and he didn't know what the fuck to do.

I didn't let on that we planned to send the police after him for what he did to Mari's finances. For now, I needed as much information as I could get so we could figure out what to do on this end.

"All right then. You got yourself in one hell of a situation and put yourself and Mari in danger. I'll take care of her, but you're gonna have to take care of yourself. Meanwhile, keep the phone, whether it's this one or another one, and stop calling Mari's phone."

"How the hell am I supposed to get a hold of her?" Brett asked.

While he and I'd been talking, I had texted my private investigator who sent back a burner number. "Here's the number to call. It goes to someone who works for me and who can get in touch with me immediately. In the meantime, lay low, and we'll be in touch."

After I hung up the call, I met Mari's troubled gaze, worry creasing her brow. "We'll figure this out. I promise."

Mari bit the inside of her cheek and wrinkled her nose as she eyed me. "Brett is such an idiot."

"I'm not gonna argue that point with you, but let's just focus on getting through to the other side of this. What were your plans for today?"

Chapter Twenty

MARI

Hannah Grantham handed me a cup of coffee, gesturing to the small tray in the center of the round table in her office. "There's cream and sugar right there. Help yourself. Just a word of warning, I do tend to make my coffee on the strong side."

She offered me a warm smile before she turned to fill her own cup of coffee from a coffee maker on a small table against the wall by her desk. I added a splash of cream and nothing else.

"Fortunately, I like my coffee strong. Thank you for taking the time to meet with me today." I took a sip of coffee, appreciating its rich, dark flavor as it slipped across my tongue.

"I'm happy to meet with you, Mari. You are giving me free press, after all." She sat down across from me. "Are you hungry? I didn't even think to ask you that. I do apologize," she said in her soft southern accent. "I can certainly see if we've got anything left over from breakfast this morning. I've got the best chef. I'm just crossing my fingers she doesn't leave."

"Oh, no, thank you. I had breakfast before I came out here."

"Excellent then. Now, before we get into what you might need for your story, tell me how you're doing."

I paused, recalling my earlier conversation with Nash. He'd suggested it was fine for me to let Hannah know what the situation was with Brett—if only to provide a level of protection for Hannah and her family. After all, she'd need to be alert in case Brett tried to stay at Creek's End Inn again.

I was still embarrassed about this entire mess. Yet, I could use someone other than my brother and Nash to shed some light on the situation.

"Well, I'm okay. It's been an interesting week," I offered.

Hannah angled her head to the side. "I'm sorry about what happened with your boyfriend. Is every-thing all right now?"

"You know how life is. Sometimes circumstances show you a person's true colors. Even if it's miserable at the time, it's all for the best in the long run. That's how I would describe what's happening with Brett."

Over coffee, I spilled the tale of what had transpired. I left out the details of what happened between Nash and me. I was still trying to adjust and absorb it.

"I'm beyond glad Nash is helping you, and of course, your brother. Between the two of them, it sounds like it will be all right," Hannah commented.

"If my brother has his way, he'll take care of it as soon as possible. I just hate this whole situation. I can't believe Brett got tangled up with a loan shark. Dear God. I would've thought it was common sense that was a bad choice."

Hannah clucked and shook her head slowly. "When it comes to money, people make dumb decisions sometimes. I sure hope you're not beating yourself up over Brett."

"I feel like such an idiot," I said with a sigh.

"Oh, hon, don't do that. Not everybody has our best interests at heart. I felt foolish once as well. I have absolutely no doubt you'll come out of this stronger and better off than before. Overbearing brothers aren't exactly helpful even when they mean well. I don't know about you, but it makes me want to show them the opposite. Nothing's worse than when they're right."

I laughed softly. "Definitely not. Thanks for listening. Nash suggested you might need to know the details if for some reason Brett thought to stay here again. I can't imagine it after he left me hanging with the bill, but this is a place he's familiar with."

Hannah didn't seem rattled. "I dare him. Don't worry about it. We're a busy place, so that should deter him. Plus, no need to worry because Alec is home for two weeks since he injured his shoulder. He's resting and rehabbing with a trainer in New Orleans."

As if Hannah conjured him, there was a light knock at the door, and it opened immediately. Alec Darrells, Hannah 's husband and basketball star, stepped through. "Just popping in to let you know I'm gonna head out to take care of a few errands. You need anything at the grocery store?"

Hannah looked over, and in a mere second, I felt as if I were interrupting a very private moment. All they did was look at each other, but the love and heat between them was evident at a glance.

"Can't think of anything, but don't you dare get Danny any more of that ridiculously sugary cereal. I'm sure he's already pestered you for it."

Alec grinned. "What if I like it?"

"It's not healthy enough for you, and your trainer would kill you," she teased as he leaned over to dust a kiss on her cheek. "By the way, this is Mari Channing. She's doing an online spread for inns around New Orleans. We're going to be in it."

Alec glanced my way, casting me an easy smile.

"Nice to meet you. I'm sure Hannah appreciates what you're doing."

"Considering she's giving me a list of recommendations, she did a lot of my work for me. Rest assured, Creek's End Inn will get top billing in the story."

After Alec departed, Hannah shook her head. "He's too much, isn't he?"

"He obviously adores you."

"I'd like to play it cool, but I adore him too," she said with a sheepish smile. "Have faith, you'll move on from Brett, and some man will sweep you off your feet."

———

Have faith, you'll move on from Brett, and some man will sweep you off your feet.

Hannah 's words echoed in my thoughts as I drove away from the third inn she'd recommended for me. Every place she'd sent me had been warm and friendly. I guessed Hannah had called every single one of them personally to smooth the welcome for me. Considering all the other stressors I was dealing with right now, I would take the help. I needed a break somewhere. If that meant a dash of kindness as I handled this one story, I'd take it.

After I drove away from my last appointment, I pulled over in a small viewing spot along the side of a country highway. It offered a view of a marshy area with cypress trees standing in the edges of the water and Spanish moss swaying lazily from the branches of trees in the early evening breeze. The sun was starting to set in the distance, casting the sky in a wash of orange and yellow mingling in the fading gold of the sun's rays.

The view was soothing, and I leaned my head against the car seat. A mere three weeks ago, I'd had no idea what was in store for me here in Louisiana. I felt as if my life had been turned upside down. I had no apartment left to move into in San Francisco, and the boyfriend I thought was trying to rekindle our relationship was now permanently gone. Somehow, I wasn't panicking about my living situation. Maybe I was acting impulsive, but—wow!—it felt good to be with Nash. Just thinking about last night sent goosebumps prickling over the surface of my skin.

Nash was unsettlingly good in bed. I kept trying to think clearly, but my brain was having a hard time getting past the haze of last night. And he was so genuine. He was going above and beyond to help me, and I didn't know what to think.

Fishing my phone out of my purse, I glanced down at the screen.

Nash: *Call me when you get this. I know you're probably working, so get to it when you can. I'd like to have your stuff taken over this evening. I've got a security team set up at the house, but I don't want to make assumptions.*

Considering that I'd already told him I was okay with staying there, I wasn't sure what his assumptions might be. Perhaps he thought it was presumptuous to move my things. Not that there were that many. I had some groceries and my single suitcase, pathetic though it was with its broken wheel.

Tapping the text screen open, I typed out a reply.

Me: *There's not much to move, so go ahead. I already packed up my clothes. Where should I meet you? I'm done for the day.*

I appreciated that Nash respected the fact that I was working. During my relationship with Brett, I wasn't often afforded that level of respect. He tended to think that since I didn't work from an office and had a fairly flexible schedule, I could simply rearrange everything related to my job on a whim.

Nash's reply came in a matter of seconds. *Meet me out at my house. Call me first though if you don't mind.*

Bemused, I tapped the button to call him. He answered on the first ring.

"Hey, how was your day?" he asked.

Dear God. All Nash had to do was answer the phone, and my body sat up and took notice with my belly spinning and every hair rising in awareness.

I didn't realize I was sitting there in silence until Nash prompted, "Mari?"

"Oh, sorry. My day went well, all things considered. How was yours?"

"Busy. Are you okay just meeting me at the house?"

"Of course. When will you be heading out there?"

"I'm on my way now, so I should be there in about ten minutes," he replied.

"Remind me of the address again."

Nash quickly recited it.

"Okay, I'll put it into my GPS." Tapping the speaker button, I pulled the phone away from my ear so I could bring up my maps and enter the address. "It looks like I'm about a half an hour away, so I'll see you shortly."

"Excellent."

The urge to offer an endearment was at the tip of my tongue. Which was ridiculous, since surely this thing with Nash was just a rebound, and I needed to remember that. And yet ...

You've got me. All of me.

Nash's words from last night kept playing on a loop in my thoughts.

I followed the friendly GPS speaker voice to Nash's house. I turned down a long, secluded driveway flanked with oak trees. The sun had fully disappeared behind the horizon, leaving nothing but fading colors as dusk settled in the wake of the setting sun.

Then, suddenly the trees opened up to a circular driveway. His home was lovely. A sprawling single-story home that blended into the landscape. It was surrounded by flowers and trees with a long porch running the length of it.

When I stepped out of my car, the air was fragrant from the heat of the day with the scents of gardenias and honeysuckle drifting around me. I didn't miss that there were two black SUV's parked to the side. I'd done a remarkable job at shoving my worries to the back of my thoughts today. Still, the sight of those vehicles brought my fear racing to the forefront of my mind.

Uneasiness prickled down my spine, and I had to remind myself I was safe with Nash. For all I knew, he'd already dealt with everything. I was lifting my hand to knock when the door swung open.

"Hey," Nash said, a slow smile unfurling across his face and sending my belly into a few spins. "Your GPS was on the nose with the time."

He held a dishtowel in his hand, which he tossed over a shoulder as I stepped through the door. The door shut behind me, and I scanned the space. We stepped into an entryway with a tile floor. Nash led me through a pair of French doors into what I presumed was the living room. Dark hardwood flooring was offset with warm, cream-colored walls. A large stone fireplace took up a wall on one side with bookshelves flanking it. On the other, a flat-screen television was mounted in the center of the wall. The entire room was inviting. It was furnished with a large sectional sofa that I imagined I'd never want to get up from once I sat down. It had soft throw pillows tossed over it and a fluffy blanket. A cream-colored rug was in the center with a dark brown coffee table just beyond the couch.

As I turned toward Nash, a dog came trotting through an archway that led into another room. The medium sized dog had white fur and a tail like a flag.

"This is Star," Nash said. "She's friendly."

Star rushed to me, circling my legs with her tail swishing against me. "I didn't know you had a dog." I knelt down to greet Star. Glancing up to Nash, I added, "I'm guessing that black star on her forehead is how she came by her name?"

Nash winked as he smiled down at us. "Good guess. Although, she's not my dog actually. She's my parents', but they have date night tonight, so they dropped her off with me for the weekend."

Straightening with a last stroke across Star's head, I couldn't help but smile. "Oh, that's too cute. Do they have date night often?"

"Every week." Nash gestured for me to follow him. We crossed the living room and walked through another archway, which opened up into the kitchen. "They have dinner together out somewhere every week. Once every other month or so, they spend the weekend out of town."

I stopped as I glanced around—the place was beautiful. Stunning really, with beautiful hardwood flooring continuing into the kitchen where a large round dining table sat within a bay window. There was just enough light left for me to see the field behind the house with a view of a river in the distance. Wooden beams crisscrossed the ceiling with a pot rack hanging above an island in the center of the room and counters lining the walls. It was clear Nash was in the middle of cooking. He walked to the island where the stovetop was and adjusted the flame under a large pan before stirring it. Star trotted across the room to curl up on the bed beside the table.

"What are we having?"

"Fresh shrimp with rice over sautéed onions and mushrooms with Cajun seasonings. It's one of my father's recipes. He told me I had to make it for you. I would've anyway, but now he's guaranteed to ask me if I did."

My heart, my confused and oh-so-tricky heart, gave a funny little thump in my chest. It was so sweet for Nash to want to make sure he pleased his father. Having seen him with his parents, the love between them was evident.

I didn't know what to make of the fact that, apparently, Nash had told his parents I would be here for the weekend. I elected to stay silent on that. My nerves were already enough of a jumble in so many compartments of my life. I didn't need to add worrying about what Nash's parents thought of me to that list.

"You're a good son, Nash," I murmured.

"I try to be. I was a bit of a wild one when I was a teenager. I've got some penance to do to make up for that."

I laughed. "I'm sure you weren't that bad."

Nash flashed a devilish grin. The sight of it had my skin prickling all over with awareness, and heat blasted me from head to toe. Nash's smiles were dangerous on their own, but throw in the naughty glint in his eyes and the sly tilt to his lips, and oh, sweet Jesus, I was in *serious* trouble.

"You have no idea. I got caught drag racing on the highway once, and I could be stubborn as hell."

My brows hitched up. "That's it? You could've been much worse."

He chuckled, the sound spinning into the need already kindling inside of me.

"*And* you cook? I think you might be too much."

Chapter Twenty-One

NASH

"Too much what?" I asked.

Mari rested her elbows on the counter opposite the stovetop where I was cooking and shook her head slowly. "Let's see. You're a wealthy real estate investor. You're handsome, and you even have a good story. To top it off, you cook."

"I have a story?" I turned off the burner under the onions and mushrooms I'd been sautéing.

"Yes," Mari replied with a slight roll of her eyes. "I can see the opening lines in the story. Local boy, born and raised on the Gulf Coast from humble beginnings. Parents are still together and keep him grounded while he makes money hand over fist. The too much is you cooking. I can already tell it's good because it smells divine in here."

I chuckled as I turned to check the shrimp in

the steamer basket. "I enjoy cooking, and my mama insisted I learned when I was growing up."

"Does your father cook?"

"Oh, yes. Both of my parents have French Creole in their roots. It's a requirement to be able to cook." I turned the burner off under the shrimp and lifted the pot to set it inside the stainless steel sink opposite the kitchen island.

"Do you need any help?"

Mari's voice was closer this time, and I turned to find that she had rounded the island. She stopped at my side, and I couldn't resist leaning over to dust a kiss across her lips. I should've known better. The moment I touched her, electricity zinged through me. Her lips were too damn tempting. They were bow-shaped, and her bottom lip was plump. When I pulled back, I was gratified to see her cheeks tinged pink, and a reluctant smile curling the corners of her mouth.

"I don't need any help, but thanks for asking," I replied.

"What goes with the shrimp?"

"Just some rolls. Now, I can't take credit for those. My mama brought the dough over this afternoon when she dropped off Star. All I did was bake them and brush them with butter."

"Can I set the table or anything?" Mari prompted.

"If you insist. Plates are over there," I said,

nudging my chin toward one of the cabinets. The cabinets had paned glass doors, so she could see where I meant. While she set the table, I got the platter with rice, onions and mushrooms ready and put the shrimp in another bowl with melted butter.

Eating with Mari was a unique form of temptation. It was simply good food, but the way she threw herself into it, well, my body definitely noticed.

"Oh my God," she said with a moan after she finished the last bite on her plate.

My mind clicked onto a memory from last night, as her body quickened just before her release. I forcibly shoved those thoughts away. If I was going to have any shot with Mari—at making her see me as more than a flash in the pan who came along at an unsettling point in her life—I needed to proceed with caution.

"Good?" I asked as I set my own fork down and took a sip of my water.

"Delicious. You can tell your father I thought it was amazing. I'm not the greatest cook. Adequate is the word I would use to describe my cooking skills."

"You don't need to be a great cook, Mari."

Her eyes snagged mine. Heat flared there, the banked embers of passion that never seemed to cool when we were near each other. Directly on its heels was a flicker of uncertainty in her gaze.

I decided a change of subject was in order. "Now

that you're not starving, let me clean up, and we can have drinks in the living room."

Mari stood quickly. "Oh, no you don't. You cooked, so I'm cleaning up. I can either wash these plates myself or put them in the dishwasher, whatever you prefer."

I shrugged as I stood and followed her over to the kitchen sink. "Dishwasher is perfectly fine." Star followed us over, and I reached into one of the cabinets to pull out her small canister of treats. I handed one to Mari. "Go ahead and give her one. She'll expect it."

Mari held the treat flat on her palm, and Star obediently sat down. She knew the drill. "Good girl," Mari said after Star gobbled up the treat.

Mari began rinsing the plates, and I called over my shoulder, "What would you like to drink? Wine, bourbon, or whiskey?"

"I'll take wine. After that meal, I need something on the mellow side."

"Red or white?" I pulled out two wine glasses and turned, resting my hips against the counter just as she leaned over to put a plate in the dishwasher. Of course, unbeknownst to her, she offered me a near perfect view down her blouse. She was wearing a loose white cotton blouse that tied in a knot at the top, paired with a flowy skirt. She was somehow both casual and business looking at the same time.

I could see the cream lace of her bra peeking out

and the curve of her breasts. I had a visceral hit of a memory—her musky scent and the way her skin felt under my lips when I swirled my tongue around one of her ruched nipples.

"White, don't you think?" Mari asked as she straightened and turned to reach for the second plate in the sink.

I'd completely forgotten my question. Martyr that I was when it came to Mari, I watched as she leaned over to put the second plate in the dishwasher. I had to curl one hand tightly around the counter, so fierce was the need pulsing in my veins. It was like a peat fire burning underground, nearly impossible to put out. Peat fires could burn for years and years.

"Nash?" Mari prompted when she straightened again and closed the dishwasher.

"White sounds perfect, nice and cool," I belatedly replied.

I released the edge of the counter and turned away to fetch a bottle of wine from the rack under the island.

"Your dishwasher is almost full," she commented. "Should I go ahead and start it?"

Filling our glasses, I kept my eyes studiously focused on my task. I didn't need to keep ogling her. "Go ahead. You can set it to run after midnight, so we don't need to listen to it."

I mentally dodged the implications of having

Mari here at my house. I'd only built this house a few years back and hadn't had a single woman spend the night here. That wasn't really something I did. I worked. All the damned time.

"Do you trust me to handle setting it?" she teased as she reached for the dishwasher soap on the counter by the sink.

I held both glasses of wine in my hands when I looked back at her. "I trust you completely, Mari."

Her question had been simple, and my answer felt weighted. Mentally brushing away that implication, I turned to walk into the living room with the wine. I heard the click of Star's claws on the wooden floor as she followed me into the living room.

Star curled up on her bed beside the fireplace. Considering I rarely used the fireplace, it amused me that was where she preferred to sleep. The day's heat was dissipating, so after I set the wine glasses on the coffee table, I crossed the room to turn off the air conditioning and open a few windows.

Mari's voice reached me just as I was opening the last window. "I do love the sound of crickets at night."

Turning, I gestured towards the sofa. "Have a seat. That's why I like to open the windows after the heat cools a bit."

Mari sat near the corner of the sectional, tucking her foot under her knee. Much as I wanted to sit immediately beside her, I kept a full cushion between us as I sat near the other end of the coffee table and reached for my wine. I nudged my chin toward the other glass. "Help yourself."

Mari lifted it and took a swallow. My eyes were immediately drawn to where she slid her tongue over the rim of the glass before lowering it. "Oh, that's delicious. What kind of wine is it? I freely admit to not being a wine connoisseur."

"I'm not either. I get whatever the place right down the street from my office building recommends. This is a Pinot Grigio. Tom, the owner, promised me it was delicious," I said with a shrug and a grin.

"I'd say Tom was right." Mari's eyes scanned the room. "This is a gorgeous space. Very mellow and not ostentatious at all."

"Did you expect it to be ostentatious?" I teased.

"Well, maybe. You are quite wealthy, so the rumors say."

"Money doesn't change who I am. Sure, I wanted a nice place and a good piece of property. But more than anything, I wanted it to be comfortable."

Mari smoothed her hand over the sofa cushion between us, her mouth curling in a slow smile. "It's definitely comfortable."

"So, tell me about today."

Mari updated me on her meeting with Hannah and her other stops. When I asked what other stories she did, she commented, "I do a bit of everything. Like I explained, I kind of ended up with this job by happenstance. I do enjoy it. It's flexible. The pay isn't the best, but at least I'm not freelancing, and I have benefits. Max would love it if I worked for him." Mari paused to sip her wine, holding it up to the light and spinning the glass between her fingers. "I don't really want to work for Max. I love him, but he can be overbearing."

"He's your older brother. I'm sure he doesn't mean to be overbearing, although I can imagine it feels that way to you."

Mari laughed softly.

"Do you think you'll keep doing what you're doing?"

Mari sipped her wine as she regarded me before lowering her glass. "For now, but not forever. At the moment, as you well know, I've got more than enough going on. Maybe once I can resolve this mess and figure out where I want to be, I'll consider other options. Meanwhile, I'll stick with it. Did you ever consider leaving New Orleans?" she asked, shifting the focus to me.

I shook my head. "No. I enjoy traveling, but this is home for me."

"It's certainly lovely. Where Max and I grew up is gorgeous too. Totally different, of course. In western Pennsylvania, it's mountains, rolling hills, and the like. My parents don't intend to stay there much longer, so there was never a draw for me to move back after college. Maybe because our hometown was so small? I don't know."

I wanted to ask Mari to consider staying here in Louisiana, which was fucking insane.

There was a sudden motion outside one of the windows. Mari jumped like a startled doe. The door-bell rang, and I stood to cross the room to the front door. One of the security guys stepped through. "What is it, Darrell?"

"Nothing to be concerned about. Just some motion in the back. I'm guessing it's a deer. If you don't mind, I think it would be best to keep the windows closed once you go to bed," he suggested.

"Of course. Makes sense. Thanks."

Darrell stepped back outside, and I returned to the living room. Mari was perched on the edge of the sofa.

"Nothing to worry about. Just a deer out back," I said. Star had stood and was pacing back and forth in front of the windows. "She might bark, but only if the deer lingers in the yard."

When I sat down beside her again, Mari sank back into the cushions with a sigh. "God, I hate this. I would like to forget I need to worry about anything."

Without thinking, I slipped my arm across her shoulders. It was a reflex, an instinct born out of protectiveness. "It's gonna be fine. I hadn't updated you yet today. I had contact with the man who runs the business where Brett foolishly took out a loan. He understands you had nothing to do with this situation, but he doesn't intend to back off of Brett."

Mari's eyes widened again, her mouth twisting to the side in a frown. "I can't believe I'm about to say this, but how the hell do we help Brett get out of this mess?"

"That's what I'm going to talk to Max about tomorrow. I want to keep security in place because we're not exactly dealing with people who operate on the straight and narrow. I don't want to create the impression that if they go after someone who matters to me, they'll get money. I'll chat with Max and sort out a plan. Meanwhile, I'm planning to go to the police station tomorrow and talk to someone I know at the precinct."

I could feel the fine tremor running through Mari and shifted my hand to move up and down her back in a slow pass. "You're gonna be fine. We'll figure this out."

Mari turned to look at me and gave a sharp nod before taking a shaky breath. "I just want to forget all of this. I feel like my life has been turned upside down and inside out. All because I dated a man who's an idiot and an asshole."

"It'll be okay."

Mari held my gaze, and something shifted in the air. The air around us felt heavy, and I became acutely aware of her closeness. I told myself I wasn't going to make a move. However, it was taking an enormous amount of willpower to hold myself in check. My need for Mari was a living, breathing force in my body. I felt coiled tight, like a spring compressed within a tiny space.

All of my restraint went up in smoke the moment Mari leaned forward and pressed a kiss—hot and gentle—on the underside of my jaw. My heart flipped in my chest, and I held myself still. "Mari?"

"I want to forget everything for a little while," she whispered, her voice husky. "You can make me do that."

As though it were a horse bolting from the gate, need claimed me and I tugged her onto my lap. Mari didn't hesitate, sliding her hand around my neck while she pressed more kisses along my jawline before she found my mouth.

I meant to take control of the moment, but it was impossible. With her tongue teasing mine, and her hand skimming down my chest between us to cup my rigid arousal, my control escaped me.

"Mari," I choked out when her lips drew back from mine before she nipped the side of my neck.

"I've got this," she teased as she shimmied off my lap.

In a few fiery seconds, she had flicked open my jeans and reached in to draw my cock out. I was already so hard, it almost hurt when my cock bounced free.

She made this humming sound in her throat. When her eyes lifted to ensnare mine, her naughty grin sent another jolt of fierce desire through me. She rubbed her thumb across the tip, where I could feel the slick moisture of pre-cum sliding over my cock head. "I love that you're this turned on," she murmured.

"It's you, baby," I nearly growled when she curled her palm around my cock, using the pre-cum to glide her hand up and down my shaft.

In a blink, she was kneeling at my feet, her dark gaze catching mine while her tongue darted out and circled the tip. My cock leaped under her touch, and I let out a rough groan as I gripped her hair when she took me in the warm depths of her mouth.

Mari sucked me in deep, swirling her tongue at the base of my cock before she drew up again. I tangled a hand in her hair, holding on as the warm suction made my cock throb. She teased, opening her eyes when she swirled her tongue on the tip again before bringing me deep. Wrapping her fist lightly around my cock, now slick from her mouth, she moved up and down, humming until the vibration nearly drew my release free.

Groaning roughly, I gripped her hair more tightly. I heard the sound of Star moving in the corner of my awareness. When Mari drew up again, I choked out, "Let's move this to the bedroom."

"How come?" she murmured as she teased her tongue around my cock head once more.

This time, I heard the click of Star's claws as she walked by the window behind the sofa. "We have an audience, and she's probably going to get curious any minute now."

The brief pause in Mari's attentions gave me a moment to grab the reins of my restraint and get a firm grip. Mari's eyes widened, and she leaned back on her heels. Straightening, she reached for my hand. "Well, lead the way then."

I tugged my jeans up as we walked swiftly toward my bedroom down the short hallway opposite the kitchen on the other side of the living room. The second I heard the click of the door shutting, I spun around. I lifted Mari in my arms and strode quickly to the foot of the bed. I held still for a moment, savoring the feel of her, warm and soft against me.

"Your turn," I murmured.

In a blur, clothes were yanked off and tossed aside in the midst of mutual kisses and greedy hands. Then, I was pressing her knees apart and dipping my head to look into the very core of her. She was restless, her hands gripping my hair as her hips rocked against my mouth. The scent of her arousal surrounded me—musky, sweet, and intoxicating.

When I sank two fingers in her channel and felt her rippling around me, I didn't wait. I swirled my tongue around her clit, giving it the slightest suction. I savored when she shuddered against me. I was aching to the point of pain as I straightened. She shimmied backward on the bed as I stretched out beside her. At the last second, I remembered a condom and reached for one in the nightstand drawer.

"Let me help," she rasped.

The feel of her light touch when she rolled the condom on swiftly was yet another sensation spinning into everything else. I was wound so tight with need, I thought I might explode.

And then, I was nudging at her slick entrance. Her legs curled around my hips, and I drove deep in one thrust. None of this was supposed to be happening. None of this was expected, most definitely not the feeling of just how incredible it felt to be with Mari.

I held still for several thundering beats of my heart as I filled her rippling sheath. When I opened my eyes, I found her lashes sweeping upward. Staring into her navy gaze, my heart spun in my chest. I felt what little control I had careening away, like a car on an icy road with no hope of stopping once the skid began.

Chapter Twenty-Two

MARI

In the dim lighting of Nash's bedroom, his eyes held mine. The look there was so intense it stole my breath and set my heart to pounding so hard every beat echoed into the next.

Emotion caught me in a riptide, its current so fierce I couldn't have stopped it if I tried. The only anchor to hold onto was Nash. So I did.

He began to move in slow, steady strokes. As he filled me again and again and again, I felt pleasure spinning faster and faster. Everything tightened in my core.

Pleasure spiraled through me faster and faster. Just when I thought I couldn't bear it any more, I chased after my sweet release. Nash reached between us. With a tease of his fingers at the very heart of me, the pleasure drew tight before snapping loose as I flew apart.

As if he'd been waiting for me, he surged inside once more, and his body went taut with a rough shout. He shuddered above me as I collapsed into the pillows, sated, and nearly limp from the depth of my release.

I opened my eyes, to find him waiting, his gaze searching mine. I felt strange, almost frightened for a moment. The intense physicality, and the intimacy of our joining spun into the tumult of emotions that had caught me in their wake.

Before I could start to overthink it, Nash was rolling to the side and holding me close. I was distantly aware of him getting up to dispose of his condom and then returning to the bed to wrap me in his strong embrace again. I drifted to sleep, warm in Nash's arms.

Despite all the insanity of my life and all the reasons to be worried and anxious, I felt completely secure and safe.

———

"Perfect!" I called as I snapped a photograph with my camera.

Elaine, the woman who owned this lovely inn, smiled as she stepped away from the pretty purple door on the old renovated farmhouse. "Do you need more photographs?" she asked as I approached from where I'd been standing in the front yard.

"I think I have enough. That's the great thing about the digital world when it comes to photography. I've taken over a hundred already," I explained with a small laugh.

Elaine smiled again. "Thank you so much for including us in this."

"You can thank Hannah Grantham. She's the one who recommended your place to me."

Elaine replied, "Hannah is wonderful. Creek's End Inn is definitely our first recommendation when we're full. It's always a pleasure to coordinate with other local business owners who support each other. Do you know when the story will be on the website?"

She followed me to my car as I opened the passenger door and set my computer tablet and camera down on the passenger seat. "I put out some feelers to several business networks here in the area to see if they'd like me to include them in the spread. My editor is checking with some print publications as well, so there's a possibility the story will be in one of those. Once we firm up the details, we'll make a decision on the timing."

Elaine's brows hitched up, and she rubbed her hands together. "Excellent. Please keep me posted and enjoy the rest of your stay in New Orleans."

"Absolutely. Thanks again, and I'll be in touch."

After I climbed in my car and drove down the winding drive, I turned off on the main road that would take me back toward downtown New Orleans. I scanned for a place to pull over to take a few minutes to check my voicemail and email on my phone.

I took an exit where there was a sign for a gas station. As I slowed to turn, I glanced in my rearview mirror and experienced a little jolt of recognition. That jolt was followed immediately by a sense of uneasiness crawling through me. I recognized the car several cars back behind me. It was also turning on its blinker to take the same exit. I'd seen the car on my way out to Elaine's inn.

It was a charcoal gray sedan. It was nondescript enough that it would be easy to assume it was a different vehicle. Yet, I recognized the license plate holder because it was bright royal blue and stood out in contrast to the gray.

With my stomach churning with anxiety, I stayed the course. I slowed and turned off when I saw the gas station. I told myself it must be nothing and filled the car with gas.

Once I was back in my car, I tucked the receipt into my wallet to turn in for work. I tapped Nash's number.

He answered immediately. "Hey, how's your afternoon going?"

"Well, everything went fine. I'm calling because I

think someone might be following me." My heart was pumping too fast in my chest, and I hated the fear coiling in my gut.

Nash's tone shifted instantly from his relaxed drawl to sharp and focused. "When did you notice this, and what does the car look like?"

I quickly summarized, ending with, "What should I do? Maybe I'm just paranoid."

"I've already texted one of the guys from the security crew at our office. He's headed out your way to rendezvous and follow you. For now, just stay right where you are. You're not in the middle of nowhere, and I'm sure there are security cameras there."

"Nash, I thought you talked to those people." I hated how squeaky my voice sounded.

"I did. But it doesn't mean they're still not gonna try to put any pressure on the situation. Sit tight, and my guy will be there any minute. Come straight to the office. I'm going to get off the phone so I can call the police station."

"Okay," was all I could manage in reply.

After I hung up with Nash, I was restless, so I called Max. My brother answered just as quickly as Nash had. "Hey, Mari, what's up?"

After I summarized the situation for him, Max swore, "Fuck. I don't like this. How are you? You know you can come out here today if you'd like."

"I know, Max. I just want this resolved. I don't

like feeling like I'm running from something that I wasn't even responsible for."

"Between Nash's contacts with his PI and the police, I think they'll be arresting Brett any day now."

"Really? Sounds like you know more than I do."

The moment that statement crossed my lips, a sense of frustration rippled through me. Max appeared to know far more than I did. I wanted to vent to him about that, but that meant potentially revealing what had passed between Nash and me. I sure as hell didn't want to do that. I could already predict Max's lecture. This time, he'd probably tell me I was moving too soon and ask me what I'd been thinking. Of course, those were my very own questions.

Just then, a car pulled up beside me, and I glanced over to see one of the security guards I recognized from Nash's office building. He gestured for me to pull in front of him.

"Max, the security guy's here, so I'll call you later."

"Got it. Call me when you can." Max paused briefly before continuing, "And sis...don't forget you can get on a plane today, if it helps you feel safer. We aren't trying to run roughshod over you."

Before I pulled out of the gas station, I didn't miss the fact that sitting on the opposite side of the street was a familiar charcoal gray car. As I drove back to Nash's office, the security guy stuck to me like a burr. I likely would never know whether it was pure coincidence or not. However, with the security detail following me so closely he was practically an extra bumper on my car, the charcoal gray sedan didn't follow me this time.

Chapter Twenty-Three

NASH

"Okay, so you're bringing Brett in this afternoon?" I asked.

"Yep. We already have his location. Considering that he's on the run from far less savory characters than the New Orleans police, my guess is he'll come in without any incident," the detective said on the phone.

"Any suggestions on how to handle the situation with the loan shark?"

The detective's laugh was dry. "Look, we have plenty of investigations going on with gangs in the area. It's constant. In your case, I can't tell you what to do. I can tell you they usually don't play dirty with people who work on the right side of the law. You have enough sway in this town that I don't think you're gonna need to worry about trouble if you decide to pay them off. They dabble in real estate and prefer not to make enemies."

"All right then. I'll think on it."

I hung up the phone just as my cell phone screen lit up. Greg was texting to let me know Mari had just entered the building.

An immense sense of relief rolled over my shoulders. When she'd called earlier, I'd almost flipped out and insisted I go out there myself. However, I knew perfectly well Greg was a good fifteen minutes closer than I was because he'd already been out running an errand.

I could acknowledge to myself that I wanted more with Mari. Yet, I was still rattled by the depth of my reaction to her and wrestling with how to handle it.

Moments later, there was a light knock on my door, and then Greg was gesturing Mari into my office. I didn't have to stand when she entered because I was already pacing in front of the windows.

When I met her eyes, I sensed something was off. I was across the room and in front of her almost instantly. "Are you okay?" I asked as I instinctively reached for her.

Mari took a step back, crossing her arms tightly in front of her chest. "I'm fine." She stared at me for a moment, two pink spots cresting on her cheeks. Her eyes were weary and unquestionably guarded.

"What's wrong?"

"Other than the fact that apparently I have someone following me? What the hell do you think is wrong?" she snapped.

While her words were accurate, I knew there was something she wasn't telling me. "What is it? There's something else."

Mari turned away, striding to the windows to stare out into the street, her arms still wrapped in front of her like a shield.

"Unlike you, I suppose I'll tell you everything. I'm frustrated because I called Max while I was waiting when you said you were calling the police. It sounds like you're keeping him more informed than me."

Fuck.

"Mari, I didn't want you to get any more stressed than necessary."

I reached her side just as she spun around. "Do you realize how stupid I feel when I learn my own brother knows more than me about what's happening?"

"Mari, if it wasn't—"

She cut in. "Look, I don't know what the hell is going on between us. I already let things go too far. At this point, I'm relatively sure that while it feels like we have more going for us, I'm obviously mistaken."

When my pulse kicked up this time, it wasn't for the usual reasons when I was in proximity to Mari. A sense of unease slithered through my veins at the distance Mari was putting between us and the admittedly annoyed look in her eyes.

"Mari, I wasn't keeping anything from you."

"Okay. How come Max knew more than me about the status of the police investigation?"

I mentally berated myself. The truth was I *had* glossed over the details with Mari, but my intentions had been good, if misguided. I didn't want her to worry anymore than she already was. "I just gave you the broad strokes. But you're right, I was more detailed with Max. Not because I was trying to cut you out, but because he's been coordinating with us on the online side of things."

Mari turned away from me again and walked to the windows. Her shoulders were stiff, and I wanted to turn her around and pull her into my arms. Somehow, I knew that was not the right move, not at this moment.

"What are we doing, Nash?"

When she turned and held my gaze, her blue eyes steely and uncertain at the same time, I knew I needed to say precisely the right thing. There was only one glaring problem—I didn't know what that was because this thing between us had caught me in its current just as rapidly as her.

"Mari, I didn't even expect to meet you. Let's just—."

Vulnerability flickered in her eyes as she lifted

her chin and pushed her shoulders back, visibly battening down the hatches around her. She took a shuddering breath, her eyes softening as she looked at me.

"You've been nothing but gracious, welcoming, and beyond helpful. There's no way I can ever really thank you for everything you've done after I unexpectedly showed up at your office. But I am coming out of a disastrous relationship. Sure, we've gotten much closer than I expected in the last few weeks, but still. My judgment leaves more than a little to be desired. I think it's best if I go stay with Max and Harlow right now."

The only way I could describe the emotion drafting through me and settling like icy cold air around my heart was fear. All of this—Mari, the way I met her, the depth of our passion, and everything tinged by the cold, dark, danger left in the wake of her ex—had me off balance. I felt as if I were on a boat during a stormy day and trying to catch my footing with waves rocking me and wind whipping relentlessly.

"Mari—" I began, starting to feel like I couldn't ever get more than a few words out when she cut me off.

She shook her head slowly. "Nash, I need some time. Within a matter of weeks, my life has been turned upside down. You have my number. I'll call you when I get to Max's."

She began to turn and walk out of my office, but I caught her lightly by the elbow. "Please stay."

"Nash, what do you want?"

"Time," I heard myself saying, realizing the minute that single word passed through my lips that it fell far short of her question.

Chapter Twenty-Four

MARI

Three weeks later

"Oh my God! You do *not* have a monopoly on making bad decisions when it comes to men," Harlow said with a hard roll of her eyes.

I looked across the table at my sister-in-law and let out a soft sigh. Harlow was awesome. I adored her. Yet, it was easy to feel intimidated by her. She was beautiful with her glossy dark hair and vibrant brown eyes. Oh, and let's not forget the fact that she was a hotshot firefighter. She was a total badass. And my brother was beyond in love with her.

"Okay, maybe I don't have a monopoly on it, but lately it feels like it. Max was completely right about Brett."

Harlow wrinkled her nose before pausing to sit for coffee. "Somewhat. He could just as easily have been wrong. Brothers seem to have a nasty habit of announcing their opinions on sibling relationships. I've told him more than once that it doesn't help at all when he butts in like that."

"How's it going, girls?" a voice interrupted.

Glancing sideways, I couldn't help my automatic smile when I saw Janet James standing there. Her silvery dark hair was twisted into a braid, and her round face was plumped up with a smile. With Harlow and Max dividing their time between Willow Brook, Alaska and San Francisco, I didn't get up to Alaska as much as I would like. I typically visited them when they were in San Francisco. The few times I'd been to Willow Brook, we always came to Firehouse Café. Janet was the owner and somehow made me feel as if she'd known me forever.

"If you want to top off my coffee, I'll take some," I said. lifting my mug and nudging my chin toward the coffee pot she held in her hand.

Janet chuckled. "That's why I carry the coffee pot around. It's amazing it hasn't attached itself to my hand. You too?" she asked when she glanced at Harlow.

"Always," Harlow replied as she flashed a quick smile. "Just put this on our tab."

Janet topped off both of our coffees. "Of course. Max just paid it off the other day."

Harlow snorted. "Of course he did. He can't help himself. I'm here more than he is, but he insists on always paying for everything. I tried to surprise him and beat him to it, but I'm not the most organized about remembering things like that."

Janet squeezed her shoulder before she turned away. "Let him take care of you, hon."

"I don't care so much about Brett," Harlow started while I added a little cream to my coffee, looping right back to where we'd been in conversation. "Tell me what the hell is going on with you and Nash."

I felt heat crest on my cheeks and bit back a sigh. Harlow knew me pretty well. Hedging, I replied, "What do you mean?" I silently prayed she hadn't shared her suspicions with Max.

"I mean, every time Max says his name, you look pretty darn interested. And, you're blushing now," she said with a pointed look.

I gulped my coffee and narrowed my eyes. "All right, if I talk to you about this, you *cannot* tell Max. I don't need to hear about it from him."

"Cross my heart." For good measure, Harlow made a cross with her index finger in front of her heart and nodded solemnly.

"Well, I guess we had a fling."

"A fling with Nash Reynolds couldn't be a bad thing. He's totally hot. I mean, Nash is not my type, but just sayin'. I have eyes. I think anyone who sees Nash would think he's pretty hot."

I rolled my eyes, but then the whole story tumbled past my lips in a rush. I ended with, "...and I don't know what to do. I think I was feeling like such an idiot after everything Brett did. It felt amazing to have someone want me. Still, I needed some space, and I didn't quite know what Nash felt for me. Plus, I figured I didn't have to worry about anything here. No one can exactly show up without getting noticed pretty quick in Willow Brook."

"Have you talked to Nash since you got here?" Harlow asked.

Harlow was clearly undeterred by my subtle attempt to change the topic back to Brett and the fact that he had a loan shark tailing me in New Orleans.

When I narrowed my eyes at her, she grinned with a sly gleam in her eyes. "I didn't miss your attempt at a detour. We don't need to discuss all that. It's been three weeks, Brett's been arrested and charged, and Max and Nash coordinated with the police to deal with that loan shark. You're in the clear and you're totally safe. Don't get me wrong, it's a good story, but not a new story for me. I'm glad you're safe, and I'm glad you're here. However, what I really want to know is what you plan to do about Nash."

"I don't know," I said, lifting a hand and letting it

fall. "And no, to answer your question, I haven't talked to Nash since I've been here. Actually, that's not true. I texted him when I landed."

"Hand me your phone." Harlow reached between us and snatched up my phone before I could respond. "What's your password?"

"I'm not telling you my password," I protested, although I didn't really care if Harlow knew it. I just didn't know what she was after.

"Fine, don't tell me. Just enter it for me."

I gave her a glare, before snatching my phone back and quickly tapping it in for her. "What the hell are you doing anyway?" I asked as I handed the phone back over.

Harlow gave me a considering look before she tapped open my messages. "Checking to see how many times Nash has texted you."

She was quiet for several moments, and then her eyes swung to mine again. "He's texted you every single day, and you're not replying."

I blew a puff of air from my bottom lip upward, forcefully blowing a loose lock of hair out of my eyes. "I don't know what to say."

"It's obvious you miss him," Harlow said when she handed the phone back to me. "Why aren't you doing something about it?"

Turning my phone face down on the table, I opened my mouth to protest, but she shook her head quickly. "Don't argue with me on that. Every time his name comes up, you whip around."

"Does Max know what you think about this?" I hedged.

"You just told me what was going on!" When I rolled my eyes, Harlow added, "I had my suspicions, and I mentioned to Max that I thought you might like Nash. But that's it. I swear. Look, take it from someone else who screwed up with men plenty, you can get past that."

I shrugged, a smile slowly stretching across my face as I regarded her. "Of course, you married my brother. Max is awesome except when he's an overbearing older brother."

Harlow snorted a laugh before pausing to take a sip of her coffee. "He is. For what it's worth, I told him no sister wants to be lectured on dating. I think you should reply to Nash and get your ass back down to New Orleans to see him. You have unfinished business." Her tone was stern and almost a dare.

"Are you serious? You're acting like this is a big thing. I seriously doubt Nash has time for an actual relationship."

Harlow eyed me and shook her head slowly. "You're scared. Look, no matter what you think about the timing, the only way to find out if this might be worth it is to try. If you don't try, you'll never know."

"The timing is *terrible*. I just broke up with Brett, and—"

Harlow cut in quickly. "You told me yourself before you even went on the trip with Brett that for all intents and purposes, you two were broken up. You'd hardly seen him for months. Plus, love isn't always about timing."

"What about love?" my brother's voice carried to us.

I cast a firm glare at Harlow. "You'd better stay quiet about this."

Max stopped beside our table, leaning over to press a lingering kiss on Harlow's cheek. As he straightened, his blue eyes flicked from Harlow to me and back again. Sometimes I hated how perceptive my brother was, so I elected to put this one on Harlow. "I was just pointing out how fast you fell for her, oh mighty brother."

Max hooked his hand over an empty chair from the table beside us to sit down quickly. "Give me all the hell you want. Harlow is the best thing that ever happened to me."

When his smile unfurled slowly, my heart clenched. "She is. Even though I was teasing, I'll never stop being happy for you."

"So, we're flying back to San Francisco in two days. Are you going with us?" Max asked.

I shrugged. "Probably. I've got to finish up that story I started in New Orleans. I have all the photographs, but I need to pull everything together. I might as well find a new place soon."

A sense of disappointment settled over me. It wasn't awful, but it was dull and tinged with regret. There was nothing to keep me in San Francisco now, except for my brother and Harlow. I wished I had a place to be, and a reason that felt purposeful and perhaps even passionate. Just like my career, my living situation and location felt like something I'd simply stumbled into. I'd gone to college there and ended up with a job, so I stayed.

San Francisco was an awesome city, and my brother was there almost every other month. Yet, there was nothing holding me there. I had friends, but I traveled enough for work that I didn't have a strong sense of belonging there.

"You know you can stay at our place as long as you need," Harlow chimed in. "We have plenty of room. Besides half the time, it's all yours."

Harlow was kind and generous, as she always was, but I didn't want to be a charity case. "I know, and I do appreciate it. I might take you up on that for the short term, but I need a plan."

"I'll cover your ticket," Max offered.

When I looked into his eyes, I knew he was just trying to be helpful however he could. I also knew the money was a drop in the bucket for him, but I hated the situation I was in. Between Nash and

Max, they'd largely dealt with the mess Brett created. Although my credit cards were back in order and so on, that didn't mean I magically had money.

"I know you will, and I appreciate it. I'll go to San Francisco and figure it out from there."

NASH

"Lydia!" I called through my open office door.

Lydia appeared in the doorway within a minute and rested a hand on her hip as she leaned her shoulder inside the door frame. "Yes?" she queried, her tone on the sharp side.

"What's the status on the closing for that property in the French Quarter?"

"It's all set. Closing is tomorrow, and your attorneys are handling everything."

I nodded and glanced back down at the screen on my laptop.

"Can I make an observation?" she asked.

Looking up, I replied, "Of course."

"I've had just about enough of your attitude. Go find Mari."

I stared at her for a long beat and then leaned

back in my chair, running a hand through my hair. "Have I been that bad?"

Lydia nodded slowly, the annoyance on her face shifting to sympathy. Which I *hated*.

"Yeah, that bad," she countered, her tone dry as chalk.

"What makes you think it has anything to do with Mari?" I hedged, rather pointlessly, but denial was a great coping skill, and I was working it these days.

"Because you've been like this ever since she left. First, you were just a little off. Then, you got snappy."

I shrugged. "Not much I can do about it because she's gone and won't reply to my texts."

Lydia considered me for a moment and then rolled her eyes. "Let me guess, you're saying vague, friendly things."

"What the hell am I supposed to say?"

"For a man who had the blessing of being raised by two parents who adore each other, you can be really clueless," Lydia said tartly as she shook her head slowly.

"What do you mean? I know I'm blessed."

"I mean your parents. Your father still gets your mother flowers for every event of the year. She's always getting him surprise gifts. I don't mean you should be getting Mari gifts, but that they do things to take care of each other in both small and big ways. They make it clear how much they love each other. I don't know how you feel about Mari, but it's obvious to me that she's the first woman I've seen who you *actually* care about."

I shrugged. "Maybe I did and do, but she thinks it was a rebound, so it doesn't really matter."

Lydia rolled her eyes again. "Don't be a typical man. At least let her know how you feel. It can't get any worse. She's already gone."

"I'll think about it," I said just as Lydia's phone rang in the waiting area to my office.

"Well, think fast." She turned and pulled the door closed behind her.

———

"Damn, I do love shrimp and grits," my father said as he leaned back and patted his stomach. Of late, he'd made a show of his aging, but he was still fit and didn't even have a belly to pat. It was completely flat.

"Always good," I agreed as I pushed my plate back and set my fork down.

My father cocked his head to the side. "What's up, Nash? You look a bit down."

I trusted my father completely, yet it still didn't feel natural to talk about this. But I'd invited him to lunch for the sole purpose of asking his advice. With that in mind, I took a breath and forged ahead.

"How did you know?"

My father's brows hitched up. "Know what? I think I'm missing part of the conversation here."

"That Mom was the one for you?"

"I didn't. Not at first. I knew I liked her an awful lot. I knew I missed her when she wasn't around. There were other factors, but I'll leave those to your imagination," he offered with a wry chuckle.

"Dear God, Dad. Spare me the details of your sex life, please."

My father shrugged. "You and your sister wouldn't be here if it weren't for that, son."

"Okay. Point taken."

"Is this about your Mari?"

"My Mari? I don't know if she's mine."

"Maybe not yet. But you two had that quality. Look, the fact you're asking me about this should give you a good hard push toward your answer. When you're wondering that much, that's a pretty strong clue. Unless you're wondering why you don't like someone very much, that's another major clue. Your mother and I just want you and your sister to be happy. We haven't had to worry as much about you because you're a man."

"Huh?"

"Men can be real assholes. If you know what I mean."

"Right," I replied, thinking of Brett and how he'd treated Mari.

"Your mother really liked Mari."

"She only met her for like a minute," I countered.

"She's a good judge of character. Over the years, I've found she's almost always right."

I interjected, "Because she is, and you're smart enough to stay on her good side."

My father winked before his gaze sobered again. "I can't tell you what to do, son. But I can tell you that I think maybe you don't wanna let Mari slide by. You just might come to regret it."

———

After I left the café—the very place I'd taken Mari to lunch the day she'd showed up at my office looking for Brett—I decided to do the next uncomfortable thing. Somehow I thought this would definitely be more challenging than my chat with my father.

"How's it going, Nash?" Max said the moment he picked up his phone.

"All right. You?"

"Busy, but that's my life all the time. Something else come up? I thought we were all done with that mess Brett made."

"We are. That's not why I'm calling."

"Oh, okay. Then, what can I do for you?"

"Do you happen to know where Mari is?" I asked, jumping straight to my point.

Max was silent for a few beats, and I could've sworn his tone was cooler when he spoke again. "I do. She's in Alaska, but she's flying to meet us here in San Francisco this afternoon. Harlow and I just flew back the other day. Did Mari leave something there?"

"Uh, no. Look, I'd really like to talk to her, and I thought I should let you know she means something to me."

I wasn't a man who experienced trepidation often, but just now, my heart was kicking against my ribs.

"Excuse me?"

"I like your sister."

Oh, fuck. *Like* didn't even come close.

"You like her? I like her too, but you're gonna need to clarify a little more than that."

"It's safe to say we definitely don't like her in the same way."

Jesus, this conversation was a fucking disaster. I didn't usually have trouble explaining anything. About now, I felt like a ten-year-old called to the front of the class when I forgot to read the assignment.

I forged on because I didn't see any other way. "Look, Mari will give me hell if I get into the details.

But I respect you. I'm coming to find her, and I hope you don't feel the need to kick my ass."

Max was dead silent on the phone, just long enough that I wondered if he hung up on me. "Max? You still there?"

"I'm still fucking here," he muttered. "Mari is coming to stay with us, and I wish I hadn't told you that."

There was a sound in the background, and then Max's voice became muffled. "For fuck's sake, Harlow. Don't—"

Next, I heard a female voice come on the line. "Nash?"

I presumed this was Harlow, but I'd only met her once and couldn't say I recognized her voice. "This is Nash."

"This is Harlow. I know Mari's not taking your calls. Here's the plan. Fly to Seattle. I'll send over Mari's itinerary, and you can meet her at the airport there."

Now, Harlow's voice got muffled before it became louder. "You can't tell me what to do. You told me yourself Nash was a great guy. Mari likes him, and apparently, he likes her, so I'm interfering. Just try and stop me."

I choked back a laugh when Harlow came back on the phone, her tone calm and smooth. "So, can you make that work?"

"Is Max okay?"

"He's completely fine. So?" she prompted.

I certainly wasn't going to argue with Harlow. "Hang on. How about you give me your number, and I'll text you once I confirm my flight?"

"Perfect." Harlow quickly recited her number, and I added it to my contacts.

"I'm gonna send a text message right now. Just reply to let me know you got it."

In a matter of seconds, her reply came through. *Text me as soon as you know your plan.*

After I finished my call with Harlow, I sat at my desk for a moment. My heart had started to kick up to a steady beat. It felt as if a ball was rolling down a hill and, truthfully, I didn't want to stop it. Now that Harlow and Max knew, I needed to see this through.

For the most part, life had been easy for me. I had parents who loved me and taught me the value of hard work and respect. In high school, I hadn't been a rich kid, but I'd been handsome and also a football star. Not good enough to go pro, but plenty good enough to get the girls. In short, I'd lead a charmed life, and that charm gave me the confidence to scrap into a real estate empire and make a ton of money even though I started with very little. I didn't mind taking risks, and I'd learned to take only smart ones.

This thing with Mari felt riskier than anything I'd done in my life. Perhaps it was because I'd never felt vulnerable like this. I wasn't one of those men who swore off romance. Rather, I simply had other priorities. And yet, just now my main priority was to see Mari. I was about to fly across the country to chase after a girl, and I didn't even know if she wanted me.

If I knew one thing, though, it was that dwelling never solved anything. With a hard mental shake, I stood from my chair abruptly and strode out of my office to stop beside Lydia's desk in the waiting area. She glanced up from her computer.

"I need a flight to Seattle. ASAP. I'd like to land by—" My eyes swung up to the clock. "—three p.m. Seattle time."

"What's in Seattle, and why so specific?" Lydia asked.

"I'm going to try to be there when Mari's flight lands from Alaska on her way to San Francisco. She's changing planes in Seattle and has a three-hour layover."

A wide smile split across Lydia's normally sober face. "I *will* find you a flight. Give me five minutes."

Chapter Twenty-Six

MARI

I adjusted the strap of my carry-on bag on my shoulder and silently cursed the fact that I'd forgotten to get a new suitcase in Alaska. That broken wheel still thumped along, jolting my wrist with every rotation as I made my way through the busy Seattle airport.

I was jostled by people, first on one side and then the other. I thanked God I had plenty of time on this layover. Airports could be a unique kind of hell. I did love people watching, but I was too tired for it today.

"Mari."

I heard my name through the low din of voices humming in the airport. The shortened version of my name was very common, so I didn't think anything of it initially. Why would I presume someone was looking for me, after all? I kept walking, although I felt the hairs stand up on the back of my neck. I didn't know why, but I sensed Nash. Stopping, I glanced around, right when I heard my name yet again. A family passed me on the left, and my view opened up.

My heartbeat took off like a rocket the second my eyes landed on Nash. He was standing in a small alcove where the various terminals met in a massive intersection of sorts. Although Nash and I were surrounded by hundreds of people, all of them intent on whatever their next destination was, it felt as if we were all alone. He pushed away from the wall where he'd been leaning. I stood stock-still in the center of the walkway until someone else bumped me.

"Jesus, lady. Get out of the way, or move," a voice said.

Whoever spoke was gone so fast I never saw them. I walked toward Nash as he approached me. My suitcase thumped and thumped behind me. Oh God, he looked absolutely delicious. His hair was mussed as if he'd run a hand through it a few too many times.

He stopped in front of me, his eyes running swiftly over my face. I stared at him numbly, trying to scramble my thoughts into something sensible. "What are you doing here?" I finally asked.

"I'm here to see you."

"You are?"

Nash's lips kicked up into a smile, and I suddenly felt giddy. Emotion rushed through me and left me tingling all over.

"I missed you," he said simply.

"You did?"

Nash nodded slowly as he reached for my suitcase and slid his other hand through my elbow. "Come on, let's get out of the way."

So startled to see him, I simply followed along. We stopped beside the windows. Planes were taking off, landing, and rolling slowly along the runways. We were surrounded by a cacophony of people—all in a hurry—as well as the rhythmic, mechanical sounds of a busy airport.

All of that faded into the distance as I looked up at Nash. I had to physically resist the urge to literally fall into his arms.

"Yeah, I did," he said.

For a second, I forgot my question, but then I remembered it. "You missed me?"

A fizzy sense of joy was buzzing in my veins just hearing Nash's voice and seeing him. My breath shortened as my heart flipped in my chest and my pulse skyrocketed.

"That's what I said. We, uh, left things kind of unfinished."

As I continued staring dumbly at him, I thought I saw a hint of uncertainty in his eyes. My heart gave a little kick, almost as if to galvanize me. "I missed you too." Butterflies lifted and spun in my belly. That was hard to say, almost scary. I glanced around us. "How did you know I was here?"

"Harlow told me you'd be landing here around now."

I started to laugh, and then alarm struck. "Oh my God, what does Max know?"

Nash shrugged. "He knows I came to find you and that you mean something to me. That's all I told him. I don't know what else he knows because I don't know what you told Harlow. I didn't dare ask her what she told him. In fact, after I heard her give him a little hell for trying to interrupt when she was talking to me, I decided it was best not to argue with her."

I threw my head back with a laugh. "Oh yeah, you don't want to mess with Harlow. She's a hotshot firefighter, and she's a total badass."

"I gathered," Nash said dryly.

Nash's hand slowly released its grip on my elbow. As my hand began to fall, he caught it in his, his grip warm and sure. When his gaze held mine, I felt warm from the inside out, almost as if the sun was cast upon my heart.

"I didn't expect you, Mari. Like I told you before, you weren't someone casual to me. Work has been my life for years, and I haven't had, or made, time to consider romance. The best part about you leaving was it helped clarify something for me."

Oh God, I'd missed his voice—that raspy southern drawl that set my heart aflutter and heat suffusing me. How could nothing more than the sound of his voice be so naughty? I didn't know, but it totally worked for me.

"I don't know what love is, but I think you might be it for me," he added.

I stared at him, trying to wrap my brain around his words while my heart kicked at my ribs as if trying to clue me into the moment. Suddenly, I burst into tears and flung myself into his arms. Hanging onto his shoulders as I wound my arms around his neck, I breathed in the scent of him—crisp with a hint of the ocean.

Nash held me tight—because he was that kind of man. His hold was warm and strong. After a moment, I shimmied down and lifted my face to his as he brushed a few loose locks of hair out of my eyes.

"I didn't mean to make you cry," he murmured, looking startled and befuddled.

I dragged my sleeve across my nose as I sniffled. "Those were happy tears. I can't say I know what love is because I've had the worst luck with men, but I think you might be it for me as well."

Nash's eyes crinkled at the corners with his smile as it unfurled slowly before he kissed me. In a matter of seconds, our tongues were tangling, and I was pressing up against him.

"Get a room!" a voice called out.

Nash and I broke apart breathlessly. We stared at each other before laughter bubbled up from my chest as he chuckled softly.

Nash reached for my suitcase again, which I'd all but forgotten. "Let's go."

"Where we going? Are you coming to San Francisco?" I asked.

"If you want me to. I was feeling confident and impulsive, so I had Lydia buy you a ticket to New Orleans. I don't know how you feel, but I don't want my first night with you in weeks to be under the watchful eyes of your brother."

"Oh, God no." I shuddered. "New Orleans sounds perfect. When do we leave?"

"Tomorrow. After a night in a hotel here." His words were perfectly tame, but the look in his eyes had sparks skittering over the surface of my skin and hot, liquid need spinning through my veins.

———

The hot press of Nash's lips on the inside of my knee felt like a drop of hot lava. Piercing pain and pleasure streaked through me as another kiss landed on the inside of my thigh.

"Nash," I gasped when he pressed his lips on the

inside of my other thigh. The sensation verged on ticklish and sent a wash of goosebumps over my skin.

"Mmmhmm?" He pressed his lips over the sensitive skin where my thigh met my hip.

"Don't make me beg," I rasped.

"Not tonight, although you deserve it after what you put me through," he murmured.

I started to laugh right when he licked my core. My laugh ended in a sharp cry. My fingers tangled in his hair as he set out to drive me crazy with his lips, tongue, and fingers.

By the time he settled his weight over me, I had begged, and begged some more. I was beyond shame and just needed him inside of me.

I felt his cock head nudge my entrance, and I curled my legs around his hips. "I need you. Hurry," I moaned.

"I'm excellent at taking orders," he murmured as he buried himself inside my channel with one swift thrust.

My need for Nash was so raw and fierce that my climax overtook me on his second stroke. It felt as if something snapped loose inside, sending piercing streaks of pleasure through me as I flew apart. I distantly heard my name in a rough shout as he followed me over the edge only seconds later.

Nash rolled us immediately over, and I rested against his chest as I tried to catch my breath. We lay still together, although I could feel the rapid pounding of his heart, thudding in tune with mine. I felt washed ashore after a storm.

When I finally lifted my head while his fingers sifted through my hair, the look in his eyes was like the sun breaking through the clouds. My heart felt as if I were basking in the sense of relief one finds after a turbulent storm. It held the sweetness of coming home.

He chuckled softly. "So much for finesse."

"Finesse?" I queried.

He nodded, his chin nudging my hair. "Yes, finesse. I told myself I was going to blow your mind. Instead, that happened so fast it felt like I was back in high school."

I laughed with him, dipping my head to press a kiss at the base of his throat. "Finesse wasn't necessary."

Chapter Twenty-Seven

NASH

A few months later, Mari looked at me from across the table in my kitchen. "Seriously?"

At my nod, uncertainty flickered in her eyes, and she looked out the window. I reached over and caught her free hand in mine where it rested on the table. "Hey, I'm just trying to let you know that I heard you when you said you didn't want to rush things."

After she looked back in my direction, a slow smile stretched across her face. "You're a good man, Nash Reynolds."

"I try."

Although we'd been spending almost every other night together, Mari was staying in the staff condo for now. I had tried to skip right past that step, but she'd insisted she needed time to settle into New

Orleans. Although I wanted to push that, time was something I had. I was going to get this right.

"I have a request, though," I added.

"What's that?"

"I want you to consider working with me."

Mari cocked her head to the side, looking puzzled. "What do you mean?"

"Your piece on the inns around New Orleans was excellent."

She cut in. "It was no big deal, just a fluff piece.

I squeezed her hand. "Do you have to knock yourself? It was really good. I ran into one of the owners at a business chamber lunch the other day. She mentioned to me that you've definitely sent some business in their direction. Although I've got a solid business here, getting it up and running has been by the seat of my pants. I've never taken the time to have someone actually plan with me regarding our website and promotional materials. I think you'd be great for that."

Mari stared at me for a long moment before another slow smile unfurled. "I might like that. As long as I'm in charge of myself. I do like to work independently."

I held my hands up. "All yours. Now, I need to get into the office."

Mari left with me, although she took her own car. She'd flown back to San Francisco and driven her car out here just last month. With Mari staying in the staff condo, we bounced between her place and my house. Part of me thought it was silly, and nothing more than an illusion to live apart. But, I knew after what she'd gone through with Brett that this was important to her. I also had enough sense to know we were still in the baby stages of our relationship. My impatience stemmed from the fact I knew, absolutely knew, I wanted to be with her completely.

Hours later, I took the elevator upstairs to her place. When she opened the door and I saw her with her hair up in a messy bun and glasses perched on her nose, I was through the door in a hot second, pressing her against it for a kiss. When I came up for air, she said, "This is stupid."

"What's stupid?" I countered, thinking kisses with Mari were anything but stupid.

"Pretending I need to stay here. I wanted to just come out to your place tonight. However, there *are* perks to having you up here for lunch," she murmured against my lips as I rested my forehead against hers with a sigh of relief.

EPILOGUE

Mari

Two years later

"And tonight's award goes to Mari Channing," the presenter announced from the stage.

Nash leaned over and whispered something indecipherable in my ear as applause broke out. I dimly felt the press of his lips on my cheek and then him nudging me up from my seat. I was in shock, but I moved automatically and walked forward.

"Mari spearheaded the renovation of several historical sections of downtown New Orleans still recovering from the damage left by Hurricane Katrina," the announcer said. "Her organization and promotion were central to this work."

I didn't even remember what I said after I received the award, but I did remember returning to my seat and being wrapped in Nash's embrace.

"See," he murmured. "I told you you're amazing."

The rest of the night was a blur where I was surrounded by friends, business acquaintances and family—in the form of Nash's parents and sister, Max and Harlow, and our parents. When I'd decided to move to New Orleans and throw common sense to the wind, I hadn't expected to land so firmly on my feet. In the time that had passed, I'd only fallen more deeply in love with Nash.

Our lives were insanely busy. Nash had meant what he said. I didn't work *for* him, I worked *with* him.

Later that night, at the birthday bash his parents and mine had organized for me out at our house, I slipped into the dress Harlow had helped me find. "Oh, it's gorgeous on you." She canted her head to the side and sighed happily.

Smoothing my hands over the creamy silk fabric that twirled around my knees and rose up in a fitted bodice, I asked, "Really?"

Harlow clasped me gently by the shoulders and turned me around. "Yes."

With my hair twisted into a knot and loose tendrils surrounding my face, my blue eyes stood out. Even I had to admit, the dress looked good.

"Now, come on," she said, slipping her hand through my elbow and walking me briskly out of the bedroom I shared with Nash. With Harlow close to six feet tall and strong, I didn't resist her tugging me along. It would've been pointless.

Moments later, I was weaving through the gardens behind our house. Nash had let me call all the shots when we'd landscaped the yard. As lovely as the home was when I moved in with him, he'd taken no time with landscaping since he'd started living there. I'd turned the yard into a lush, fragrant garden. The scent of gardenias in bloom drifted through the air mingling this evening.

I paused beside Max. His blue eyes twinkled as he smiled down at me. "Good work, Mari."

"Thanks, Max. It's been fun. Who knew I'd be so good at this?"

"I did." His gaze had gone dead serious.

I smiled softly. "I landed in the right place."

"You did," he replied with a nod. "Nash is looking for you, by the way." He nudged his chin through the crowd to where Nash stood on the edges.

I leaned up and pressed a kiss on my brother's cheek. "Well then, I guess I'll go find him."

Nash still took my breath away. He had tossed off the suit jacket he'd been wearing earlier and rolled up the sleeves of his shirt. This showed off his muscled forearms, which I totally had a thing for.

Stopping in front of him, I commented, "I heard a rumor you were looking for me."

His hazel eyes locked with mine, and for the thousandth or more time, I felt as if I were all alone in the world with him. It didn't matter that we were in a crowd. My breath hitched in my throat when he leaned over to brush his lips across mine.

"I'm always looking for you," he murmured.

NASH

Music played softly in the background as the night wore on, and I searched out Mari once again. We kept getting pulled apart by the various demands of our guests. I didn't mind being social and had the manners to get through it, but damn, I was ready for this night to end so I could have her all to myself.

My eyes landed on her back. Her shoulders were exposed in this gorgeous cream silk confection she was wearing. Her bronze skin glinted under the lanterns circling the garden.

"Here you are," I murmured from behind as I slid my hand around her waist.

She smiled at me, her blue eyes almost navy in the dim light. "And there you are."

I couldn't wait any longer.

Looking into her eyes, I kept my hold on her with one arm as I slipped my hand into my pocket. Conveniently, Mari didn't notice because she threw her head back in a laugh when the band said they were dedicating the next song to her.

The band was a regular at Johnny's Bar. While we didn't frequent any bars, Johnny was an old friend and we did occasionally go there for drinks and business. The band had come to know Mari loved old blues music and usually dedicated random songs to her.

She met my eyes again, her gaze laughing. "They're ridiculous."

I shrugged, leaning over to drop a kiss on the side of her neck because she was too tempting. "So tell me something," I began as I lifted my head.

"Anything," she said swiftly, her tone light and teasing.

"Now, don't you go promising me the world until you know what I want."

While I was teasing too, my heart felt like it was going to split at the seams. Mari did that, made me feel so full of love it almost hurt. Loving her was always like walking along that knife's edge of pleasure and pain. Because it felt so good, and yet she had so much power to cause me so much pain.

"What is it, Nash?"

"Well, I was wondering if you'd marry me."

I'd never wrestled this much with my feelings. I rarely worried about rejection. But then, when there wasn't anything that mattered on the line, there wasn't much to worry about.

Yet, right here, right now, my heart pounded harder than I'd ever experienced and holding myself steady as I waited for her answer was another form of agony. I knew Mari loved me, but I didn't know just yet if she was ready to cross the line into promising forever.

Her eyes widened, and her breath hitched in her throat as she took a sharp inhalation. "Oh! I wasn't ready," she gasped, her voice raspy.

I held steady inside, although my stomach clenched in response to that. "Ready for what?"

"Oh, don't you worry, Nash," she said as she slid her hand up to cup my cheek. "I'm ready for forever with you. I just wasn't expecting the question tonight. I had it all planned out how I was going to say yes. I was even thinking I might have to ask you because you're taking your sweet time, as usual."

My heart did split wide open then, and a sense of unbearable joy filled my chest. Somehow, she always managed to say the perfect thing. "I *do* like to take my time."

My tendency to take it slow was a joke between us. She was prone to getting impatient when we were making love or fucking like crazy wherever we happened to be.

"Yes, yes, yes, yes." Each word came out stronger, and her eyes glittered with tears as I opened my palm. The ring that had been practically burning a hole in my pocket was now held there.

"Oh, oh," she breathed. "It's gorgeous."

My mother had given me my grandmother's

wedding ring a few months back, and I'd been waiting for the exact right time to ask. It was a white gold band set with a sapphire that matched Mari's eyes. According to my mother, she was supposed to give it to me when I found the right woman.

Then, I was sliding the ring on Mari's finger and lifting her against me as we spun in a circle. At some point, someone figured out what was happening, and we were surrounded by well-wishers.

Hours later, the party had dispersed from our garden. Mari sat with me on a bench between an oak tree and a flowering gardenia. The moon was hazy through the clouds drifting above us, and the stars winked brightly from light-years away. Mari's legs were draped over my lap, and her head was tucked against my shoulder.

My fingers sifted through her hair, and my voice was quiet in the darkness. "I didn't plan on a public proposal."

"It was perfect," she said as she lifted her head. "What now?"

"Well, now I'm impatient. I think we should go to the courthouse tomorrow."

"Did you forget tomorrow's Saturday, Nash?" Her lips kicked up a small smile when she lifted a hand and traced her fingertips along my jawline.

"Monday then. I can wait two days."

Mari giggled and leaned forward. Her lips landed

in a soft, open kiss on the side of my neck. "For once, you're in a hurry."

"When it comes to forever with you, I am *absolutely* in a hurry."

With that, my almost-wife climbed onto my lap and made me forget everything but the moon, the stars, and her.

Thank you for reading Mari & Nash's story! Sign up for my newsletter, so you can receive information about upcoming new releases & receive a FREE copy of one of my books: http://jhcroixauthor.com/subscribe/

If you'd like to meet Mari's brother, Max, check out Melt With You - Harlow & Max's holiday story. A tech billionaire collides with a sassy firefighter heroine - opposites attract doesn't quite capture it.

If you haven't read any of the other stories in that series, you can start with Burn For Me, a second chance romance for the ages. Sexy firefighters? Check. Rugged men? Check. Wrapped up together? Check. Brave the fire in this hot, small-town romance. Amelia & Cade were high school sweethearts & then it all fell apart. When they cross paths again, it's epic - don't miss Cade's story!

For more swoon & sass...

This Crazy Love kicks off the Swoon Series - small town southern romance with enough heat to melt you! Jackson & Shay's story is epic - swoon-worthy & intensely emotional. Jackson just happens to be Shay's brother's best friend. He's also *seriously* easy on the eyes. Shay has a past, the kind of past she would most definitely like to forget. Past or not, Jackson is about to rock her world. Don't miss their story!

For more small town romance, take a visit to Last Frontier Lodge in Diamond Creek. A sexy, alpha SEAL meets his match with a brainy heroine in Take Me Home. Marley is all brains & Gage is all brawn. Sparks fly when their worlds collide. Don't miss Gage & Marley's story!

If sports romance lights your spark, check out The Play. Liam is a British footballer who falls for Olivia, his doctor. A twist of forbidden heats up this swoon-worthy & laugh out loud romance. Don't miss Liam & Olivia's story.

Be sure to sign up for my newsletter for the latest news, teasers & more! Click here to sign up: http://jhcroixauthor.com/subscribe/

6) Like my Facebook page at <u>https://www.facebook.</u>
<u>com/jhcroix</u>

Wild Fire Series
 All The Afters
 When We Dare
 Fake It True
 Only Ever You
 Just For Us - coming 2026!
 Heartfire Falls Series
 What We Keep - due out August 2025!
 Mine To Hold - coming 2026!
 Fireweed Harbor Series
 Make You Mine
 Dare To Fall
 Be The One
 One More Time
 Wait For You
 Ever After All
 Light My Fire Series
 Wild With You
 Hold Me Now
 Only Ever Us
 Fall For Me
 Keep Me Close
 With Every Breath
 All It Takes

Take Me Now
Meant To Be
Dare With Me Series
Crash Into You
Evers & Afters
Come To Me
Back To Us
Take Me There
After We Fall
Swoon Series
This Crazy Love
Wait For Me
Break My Fall
Truly Madly Mine
Still Go Crazy
If We Dare
Steal My Heart
Into The Fire Series
Burn For Me
Slow Burn
Burn So Bad
Hot Mess
Burn So Good
Sweet Fire
Play With Fire
Melt With You
Burn For You
Crash & Burn
That Snowy Night

Haven's Bay Holiday Series
All I Want
All I Need
All We Have
All We Are
Brit Boys Sports Romance
The Play
Big Win
Out Of Bounds
Play Me
Naughty Wish
Diamond Creek Alaska Novels
When Love Comes
Follow Love
Love Unbroken
Love Untamed
Tumble Into Love
Christmas Nights
Lodge Series
Take Me Home
Love at Last
Just This Once
Falling Fast
Stay With Me
When We Fall
Hold Me Close
Crazy For You
Just Us

ABOUT THE AUTHOR

USA Today Bestselling Author J. H. Croix lives in a small town with her husband and two spoiled dogs. Croix writes contemporary romance with sassy women and alpha men who aren't afraid to show some emotion. Her love for quirky small-towns and the characters that inhabit them shines through in her writing. When she's not writing, you can find her cooking, counting the birds in her backyard, and running with her dog, which is when her best plotting happens.

Places you can find me:
jhcroixauthor.com

faccbook.com/jhcroix
instagram.com/jhcroix
bookbub.com/authors/j-h-croix

* 9 7 8 1 9 5 4 0 3 4 8 3 9 *